Let love SHINE

BOOK 3.5 IN *THE LOVE* SERIES

by Melissa Collins

LET LOVE SHINE

Copyright © 2014 by Melissa Collins

All rights reserved

ISBN-13: 978-0-9910542-2-0

ISBN-10: 0-9910542-2-9

Cover design and graphics by Sommer Stein with Perfect Pear Creative and Toski Covey Photography

Interior Design by Integrity Formatting

Edited by Becky Johnson Hot Tree Editing

Dedication

For those who find simple moments of beauty in their otherwise chaotic lives.

Summer
August 2013

PROLOGUE

Maddy

"Okay, sweetie. It looks like you're all set to go." The nurse smiles warmly at me as she hands me my discharge papers. Looking over at Reid, she asks, "Why don't you bring the car seat up to the room and pull your car up front. It'll be easier to load the little guy in his seat in here than it will be in the car." She tips her chin to the bassinette in the corner where Braden is napping.

Reid nods politely, but I see the scared-shitless look on his face. I'm sure there's a similar one on my face too. We're going home with our baby today. That'll scare the crap out of anyone.

As he walks past me, he kisses my forehead. "I'll be right back up." The nurse walks out with him telling him where to park the car so it won't be towed, and explaining how to remove the seat.

I remember a few weeks ago when we tried to install the car seat ourselves. Standing in the sweltering summer heat, trying to tell Reid the instructions as he was all contorted and twisted in the back of the Jeep was *so* not fun. In the end, we got too frustrated and concerned that we were going to mess something up, we ended up driving to the local fire station where they installed it for us.

That sucker is good to go, now.

I scoot off the bed and wince only slightly as I stand. Luckily, everything about my delivery went smoothly and I was only required to stay in the hospital for two nights. But, a smooth delivery does not mean a pain-free one, so I can't help but wince slightly as I pad over to where Braden lies sleeping.

Lightly grazing my fingers over his head makes him squirm slightly. Blinking his big, blue eyes as he wakes, I feel my heart swell with love. "Hey, baby boy. Did you have a good nap?" He stretches his arms out of his swaddled blanket and yawns. Sliding my hands under his arched back, I lift him and hold him so his head rests under my chin. Inhaling the sweet, baby-fresh smell of his hair, I kiss him and whisper, "I love you, little man."

Easing us down into the chair causes me to wince once more, but with Braden in my arms, nuzzling against my chest, I barely notice the pain. As he falls back asleep against my chest, I feel complete.

I know this is my purpose in life.

For as long as I can remember, I've wanted nothing more than a family of my own. Now, I have it. There's nothing else in this world that could make me happier. There will always be a part of me that wishes my parents could be here to share this part of my life with them. But, in the last year or so, I've learned how to make peace with their passing. It wasn't easy and I wish I hadn't spent so many years in the dark over it, but with Reid and now Braden lighting my days, the pain of them no longer being with me has lessened drastically.

"Now, there's something I'll never get tired of seeing." Reid's voice rouses me from my day-dreaming. He walks into the room and places the car seat on the bed. Squatting on the floor in front of us, he brushes my hair back out of my eyes and tucks it behind my ear. Nuzzling into his hand, I kiss his palm.

"Thank you for taking care of me last night." He shoots me an 'are you kidding?' look.

"Maddy, I live to take care of you. And now, I live to take care of him too." Reid stands in front of me and opens his arms for me to hand him Braden.

After he buckles Braden into his car seat, Reid turns back around and helps me get out of the chair. "Yeah, but taking care of me doesn't usually involve brushing my hair."

"Maddy, you had just given birth to our son and your hair was all over the place. You wanted it taken care of, so I took care of it. It's that simple." I wrap my arms around his waist and press my cheek up against his solid chest. Inhaling the scent that is so uniquely Reid, I know he is my knight in shining armor. "I don't know what I did to ever deserve you," I mumble against his T-shirt.

Pressing his lips to my forehead, I feel his smile. "Yeah, you did get pretty lucky, huh."

"You know, you didn't make out half bad either." I arch an eyebrow at him as I lean back from our embrace slightly.

Reid scans my face as if he's searching for the lost city of Atlantis or something like that. "Yeah, I guess I'll keep you." The dopey, lopsided grin plastered to his face makes me laugh, which of course, is still a bit painful. As I wrap my arm around my still more-than-slightly-rounded belly, a small hiss of pain slips past my lips.

Concern replaces his smile. "Shit, I'm sorry, babe. Are you okay?"

When the flash of pain passes, I wipe a bead of sweat from my brow. "Yeah, I'm good. Just still a little sore." The muscles in my belly are still crazy sore from pushing and I've got a handful of stitches in places I never thought to have them. "Just no more laughing, okay?"

"You got it. I promise. I will never make you laugh again." His cheeky response earns him an eye roll and a small, but much less painful, laugh. "Come on. Let's break this kid out of here and go home." Reid clicks the car seat handle in place just as the nurse walks into the room with my wheelchair.

"Are you guys all ready?" She folds down the legs and pats the seat for me to sit in.

"Yep, we're all set." Reid's words are filled with so much happiness and pride; it makes a face-splitting smile pull at the corners of my lips.

I have this distinct memory of the first time I ever rode in Reid's new Jeep. I envisioned him driving home from the hospital, with me and the baby next to each other in the backseat. I pull the seat belt across my lap, and rest my hand across Braden's chest. This is the most perfect moment of my life.

We're going home today as a family.

My family.

Our family.

A stray tear rolls down my cheek. It's one produced of pure happiness. Reid peeks back at us through the rearview mirror, and even though there are no tears in his eyes, I know he feels the same way I do right now.

Complete.

When we pull up to our apartment fifteen minutes later, I catch sight of the wooden stork announcing Braden's birth staked to our small patch of front lawn.

"Don't look at me," Reid says defensively. I told him that I didn't need a whole bunch of fanfare over me coming home or anything like that. As proud as I am of my little family, I'm still a nineteen-year-old, who had to drop out of college because she got pregnant. It may be silly, but there's still a part of me that feels ashamed.

Reid twists to face me in the backseat. "It was all Momma and Mel. And you know I didn't have a chance in hell at stopping them."

He's right. It's possible that those two might be more excited about this baby than we are.

Yeah, they're *that* excited.

Which explains why they're already here to greet us as we begin unloading the car. "I got it, Maddy." Melanie grabs the bag from my hands and hugs me to her side. I love that she came home just for me. She just moved into her own off-campus apartment with the girls. It's weird that we're both going down very different paths now. Yet, no matter how far apart it may seem like our lives are drifting, we'll always be there for each other. I know this with absolute certainty.

"Thank, Mel. You guys didn't have to be here. You know that, right?" Yeah, that goes over like a lead balloon with Momma who pulls a face at me from behind Melanie.

"You're right, Maddy," Momma quips and smiles at me. "We don't *have* to be here, but a freight train couldn't keep us away."

With their help, we manage to get everything unloaded from the car – flowers, baby gifts, our bags and, of course, our son.

We walk Braden into his nursery and change his rather stinky diaper. We're still not great at it and he wiggles so much, that within a minute, I've got poop smeared on my hand and I feel like I'm going to damage him in some way. Reid's no better. Who would have ever thought it would take two adults to change the diaper on a six-pound baby?

We must've done something wrong, because when we're just about done Braden gives his lungs a whirl and screams like a banshee.

I snap his onesie and pull him into my arms. "Shh, little guy. It's okay." Reid stands next to me, his hand on my back for support, but I feel like a failure. I can't even change my son's diaper without him crying. And now, he just won't stop.

Great.

As if she senses my frustration, Momma pokes her head into the room. "You okay in here? Can I help?"

It's as if her question opens a flood gate. I lose it. "I was just trying to change him…he wouldn't stop moving…I got crap all over…then he started screaming…I…"

Damn hormones.

Rubbing calming circles on my back, Reid coos into my ear. "It's okay, baby. You did great."

"He's right, Maddy. Besides, you'll get the hang of it and be able to change a diaper one-handed in no time." I don't know why I originally thought I didn't want anyone here when we got home. Where would I be without Momma?

"Thanks, Momma. What do we do now?" Reid and I look over to her like she's holding the Holy Grail. Yeah, we feel that clueless right now.

"I think you could both use a little nap. Let me take him off your hands." Cuddling Braden in her arms, she's all too eager to play grandma for a little bit. "Reid, go get Maddy some Advil and you should both get some rest. You're going to need it if you plan on making it through the night." Well, those words make my gut churn with nervousness. Maybe some pain meds and sleep aren't such a bad idea, after all.

I'm not sure if it's the sight of my own bed, or the thought of cuddling up with Reid, or the knowledge that Momma is taking care of Braden, but the second I step into our room, exhaustion washes over me. Reid steps behind me and very gently wraps his arms around my not-so-skinny waist. "I'm so proud of you, Maddy."

"Me? For what? Not snapping our kid's leg off while I was changing him?" I scoff sarcastically. Seriously, I hope it gets easier.

"Yeah, there's that." He pops a sweet kiss on my temple before turning me around to face him. "But mostly, I'm proud of you because you're amazing and that baby is going to love you so much, no matter how horrible you are at changing his diaper."

I snuggle into him and thank God that I have Reid by my side. When he feels me yawn against his chest, Reid moves to the dresser and pulls out one of his T-shirts. "Arms up, Mommy." He grins goofily at me, but I welcome his help getting changed. Then, we curl up together in bed and fall asleep almost instantly.

*****

Sometime later, a gentle tapping on the door wakes me from my sleep. "Someone's hungry." Reid stands from the bed and Momma hands Braden to him. I push up in bed and situate myself so that I'm comfortable. The nap and the Advil worked wonders for me and moving is becoming a little less difficult—for now, at least.

"I'll leave you guys alone. Melanie and I are going to run to the store and pick you up a few things. We'll be back soon." She waves from the doorway and Reid slides into bed next to me. He puts a pillow on my lap and helps me get Braden in the right position. When he's all latched and ready to go, Reid wraps an arm around my shoulder.

"I love you," he whispers into my ear as he stares amazed at his nursing son.

By the time Momma and Melanie make it back from the store, Reid, Braden and I are in the living room lounging on the couch.

Reid moves to help Momma with the bags and Melanie sits down next to me. Reaching for the baby, I pass him over into her arms. Staring down into in his cute-as-a-button face, Melanie smiles and I see tears building in her eyes. "He's so beautiful, Maddy. I can't believe you're a mommy." She reaches over and laces her fingers through mine.

"And you're an aunt and Godmother too." I drop that last piece out there, but it really shouldn't be a surprise.

"Really?" she gasps and covers her mouth with the hand that's not currently cradling Braden to her chest.

"Of course, Melanie. You're the only sister I'll ever have and the only aunt he'll ever have." The tears that were building spill over and down her freckled cheeks.

"Thank you so much, Maddy. I…" Her words disappear behind her happiness and we sit together chatting about nothing while Momma and Reid make dinner.

"Thank you for dinner, Momma. It was perfect." I lean back in my chair as I finish my last bite of pasta.

"Of course, sweetie. We all know how well you and that kitchen get along." I stick my tongue out at her, but she's right. I can't cook to save my life. Standing from the table to clear the dishes, Momma adds, "Now, there's plenty of leftovers in the fridge and I'll stop by tomorrow with a few more dishes you can put in the freezer." The woman is seriously sent by God.

After dinner is all cleaned up, Momma and Melanie get ready to leave. Hugging me tightly, Momma kisses my cheek. "If you need anything at all, please don't be afraid to call me." Looking between Reid and me, she adds, "No matter what time, understand? I can be here in five minutes if you need me."

"Thank you, Momma. We will." Reid hugs her and Melanie goodnight and softly closes the door behind them.

We sink down onto the sofa and enjoy the silence that we know won't last very long. Looking up at the clock, Reid says, "He'll probably want to eat in about a half an hour." He pulls me to his side and I relax into his body. Clicking on the television, he starts flipping through the channels before settling on SportsCenter.

"The apartment feels different now, doesn't it?" I ask as he's lightly tracing circles on my upper arm. The motion is hypnotically soothing.

"It does. He makes it feel different. It feels like a home, now." Reid plants a soft kiss on the top of my head, and as if he can tell we've just gotten comfortable, Braden starts crying from his room.

Reid stands and helps me up from the couch. "You ready for this, Mommy?"

"Nope, not a bit, but I've got you, so it's all good." He wraps his arm around me and we walk down the short hallway to take care of our son.

I won't lie; the night didn't go perfectly. Tears were shed—and they weren't all Braden's. We may have gotten only about three hours of sleep, but we survived. It may not have been pretty and God knows it wasn't stress-free, but we did it together. And that's how I'll always remember it.

Summer
August 2014
- One Year Later -

CHAPTER ONE

Reid

"Hey, babe," I call out as I toss my keys on the sidetable by the front door. Dropping my messenger bag to the floor, I loosen my tie as I glance at the pictures next to me.

The framed smiles of my mom and Shane stand proudly on the table. After we moved in, Maddy finally decided to go through a few boxes of pictures that her Aunt Maggie left for her when she died. So now, mixed in with pictures of our happiest memories—the day Braden was born and the day we were married—are now pictures of Maddy and her parents from her childhood. Nestled in between all of the people who are most important to us, stands the jar of sand from the beach in Montauk. They might not all be with us physically, but in spirit, our families are still very present in our daily lives.

I hear dishes clattering and the garbage pail being slammed shut from inside. Hearing her muffled curses makes me laugh. Something is obviously stressing her out, so I make my way into the kitchen to check it out. Wrapping my arms around Maddy's waist from behind, I pull her close to me and inhale the sweet scent of her hair.

Then, I catch sight of the kitchen.

"Did a tornado blow through here or something?" I kiss the top of her head and feel her sag against me.

On an exasperated sigh, she huffs, "No, there was no tornado. Just me thinking I could actually bake our son his first birthday cake." That explains the flour dusted across her forehead, which I now notice as she turns to face me.

I can't stifle the chuckle. "You should have known better, Maddy. You and this kitchen are enemies." That comment earns me a smack to the arm.

"Why don't you just order something from the bakery? You know, like I suggested a few weeks ago."

Flopping into a chair, she takes stock of the kitchen. "Yeah, maybe. But I just want to try one last time. It's important to me for some silly reason."

"Sweets, it's not a silly reason." I squat down in front of her and lift her chin. "You're an amazing mom. I love that you want to make it as special as possible." I pop an innocent kiss to her lips and feel her smile. "Now, what can I do to help?"

Just as she's about to tell me what to do, Braden giggles from his nursery. "Do you think you could take him out to the park or something for a little bit so I can figure this cake situation out?" she asks hopefully.

I kiss the tip of her nose. "You got it," I say as I swipe my thumb across her cheek where a bit more flour is dusted. Taking one last glance at the mess spread out across the counters, I think maybe I should place an order with the bakery just in case.

"Hey, little man." Braden is sitting in his crib playing with a stuffed animal, but when he hears my voice, he quickly pulls himself up using the railings and reaches for me to pick him up. Nuzzling into my chest, I squeeze him tightly. "What'd you do today, buddy?" His response of bubbles and coos is all I need to smile and laugh. "Really? Well, it sounds like you've had a rough one. Want to hit the park with me?" He's only one, but I swear, when he hears the word park, he looks at me like I just asked a dog to go for a ride in the car. Wiggling in my arms, I can tell he's excited about it.

"Okay, okay. Let's go then." I grab a few things and make my way back into the kitchen, where I catch the tail end of Maddy's phone call.

"Who was that?" Braden reaches for Maddy grunting for her to hold him.

Reaching for Braden in return, she says, "It was Mel. She's coming over to help me."

"Oh, I see how it is. Daddy's fine until Mommy's in the same room." Maddy rolls her eyes at me as I hand her Braden. "Does Mel's 'help' involve a bottle of wine like it did last time?" I quirk an eyebrow at her and she sticks her tongue out at me, but she doesn't answer.

She starts bopping up and down as she sings some silly song. Braden's laughter fills the room. Maddy twirls around with him and his smile is infectious. So is hers. Maddy, with our baby on her hip, is a sight I'll never get tired of. It makes me realize just how far we've come and how happy we are.

Sure, we're exhausted most days, but it's all worth it. This past year has definitely been the most trying in my life, but we've survived our first year as parents. I still remember that first night at home. It was hell—pure and utter torture. I was convinced Braden was possessed by some evil spirit sent here to keep us awake for days on end. Maddy had a bit of a rough recovery and was sad most days. Those days were the worst. Momma spent a lot of time here helping Maddy figure things out. We struggled a lot and fought more than I care to admit, but we decided anything that happened between the hours of 10 p.m. and 8 a.m. didn't count. Eventually, Braden learned how to sleep through the night and we started getting some more sleep too. It's amazing what you can accomplish on only four hours of sleep, but parenthood—added to working or going to school full-time—isn't for the faint of heart.

This shit is serious work.

Yet, here we are a year later and we couldn't be happier to have Braden's first birthday party tomorrow with our friends and family. Between prepping for the party, me working overtime, and Maddy finishing her last summer course, we've barely been able to stay awake past eight every night.

But watching them dance and laugh in front of me makes it all worth it.

I pull them both into my arms and just hold them for a quick second before Braden starts shimmying out of Maddy's arms. He's caught sight of his Lightning McQueen racecar on the floor and is reaching for it. Handing him his car, Maddy puts him in his bouncy seat. The sight of my wife taking care of our son, talking baby talk and kissing him sweetly should warm my heart. But all I can see is her ass right now. Yep, I want her.

"Get over here." I pull her back to me once Braden is situated and brush her hair out of her eyes. "You look beautiful, you know that?" I trail sweet, soft kisses behind her ear and down her neck.

"Hmmm," she mumbles and it makes me smile against her skin.

Moving from her neck across to her mouth, I feel her lean into my lips. This is something else of which I'll never get tired. Her full, luscious lips pressed against mine; the taste of her sweet mouth still drives me crazy. "Well, hello there." Pulling away from our kiss, Maddy arches her eyebrows as she presses her hips into my groin. The last motion surprises me more than a little. To say that our sex life has been different in the last year is, well, it's an understatement to say the least.

"What? I'm not allowed to want my wife." I grab her ass and push her into my erection a bit more. Our hands roam as the kiss rises in intensity. I fist a handful of her hair and pull her mouth even closer to mine. It's the hottest kiss we've had in a while. Just as her hips start to roll into mine, we're distracted by a sound, and smell, to which we've grown all too accustomed in the last year.

Before I can even move my hands from her body, Maddy's pinching her nose closed. "Not it!" She calls out and laughs.

"Damn, you're getting quick!" It's kind of been our thing to decide who gets to change him. I scowl playfully at her and she just laughs at me.

"Dude, you're killing my game." Braden smiles as I hold him out in front of me. "Holy crap! What the hell did you feed this kid today?" Seriously, he's lethal.

"He ate the same as usual. He's just a stinky little monster." She says the last sentence to Braden in that ridiculous baby talk. You can talk sweet about it all you want; it's still poop.

By the time I'm done changing his diaper and changing out of my work clothes, Melanie and Bryan are walking through the door.

"Hey, little man. Aunt Melly missed you, you little booger." She grabs Braden out of my arms and blows a raspberry on his round cheek.

"What? No love for me?" I shoot her a look of feigned insult as she shoves a grocery bag, filled with what I'm assuming is cake-making supplies, into my hands.

"Nope, sorry. You're not cute enough." She doesn't even look at me as she bounces Braden around laughing with him. I can't argue with her. He is pretty adorable.

"Don't look at me, man." Shifting all of the bags to one hand, Bryan extends his hand for me to shake. "Even *I* can't compete when Braden's around."

Bryan walks into the kitchen to put down a few more bags of groceries and I can't help but wonder what the hell kind of cake she plans on baking.

Maddy walks up next to me and wraps her arm around my waist. Stretching up on her toes, she whispers in my ear, "I'll pay you all the attention you want later." She quickly nibbles on my ear lobe and the erection I had managed to calm is back.

"I'm going to hold you to that, you know." I run my nose along hers and kiss her softly. "No passing out on me like last night."

"It's a date, baby." Her eyes are so wide I can see the golden flecks in her green irises. Maybe she's as excited about it as she used to be.

"Okay, hand him over. You girls go do your thing." I hand Melanie back the last bag of groceries and laugh as she pulls out the bottle of wine I knew she'd have with her. Yeah, because being tipsy is what's going to help Maddy cook better.

Maddy and Melanie's giggles filter back out into the living room and Bryan looks more than a little afraid to stay behind. I can't blame him. Those two together with wine and chocolate—nothing good will come of that.

Slinging the diaper bag over my shoulder and grabbing my car keys, I clap my hand on Bryan's shoulder. "Don't worry; you can come with us."

"Thanks. You sure they'll be alright?" he asks as a pan crashes down to the floor.

"Yeah, they're good, but we should stop and grab some take-out just in case."

*****

With dinner in one hand and an exhausted toddler in the other, we return home to a living room filled with girlish laughter. Maddy and Melanie are sitting next to each other on the couch chattering over some tabloid-like "news" show. They're so engrossed over what they're watching, they barely look up from the screen. I catch bits of the story—something about some book-turned-movie that's coming out this winter. They've been buzzing over it for months now—years is more like it. I've already been told that I'm on baby duty that night, but if the pay-off from the movie is half as good as the pay-off from the book, then I'm more than fine with that.

I strap Braden into his high chair and give him some Cheerios to keep him occupied while Bryan and I get the stuff ready for dinner.

"Hey, are you and Dylan still getting that league together?" Cheerios fly in the air and Bryan squats to get them.

"Yeah. Why? You think you want to join?" I mentioned it to him last week, but never really thought he'd be interested.

"I mean, I'm more of a soccer player than slow-pitch softball, but yeah, if there's a spot, I'll take it." He shrugs his shoulders and leans back against the kitchen counter. The air around him suggests he wants to seem disinterested, but from what Melanie tells Maddy, and then in turn, what Maddy tells me, Bryan misses being part of a team; there's only so much high-fiving and nice-job ass slapping that you can get away with in a computer lab.

"Cool, man. I'll let Dylan know and I'll get you a jersey on Monday." We exchange a quick nod and lightly tap fists before we finish getting dinner ready.

"Dare we disturb their book boyfriend news story?" I ask as I start opening the containers of Chinese take-out.

"Nah, they'll smell the food eventually. I doubt they even realized we walked in." He laughs as he peers back out into the living room where the girls are still glued to the image of some guy in a suit on the screen. "What's he got that I don't, huh, Melanie?" Bryan's words pull her attention away from the screen—marginally.

"Him?" She barely even looks up at Bryan. "It's simple really. He's got a red room of pain! Is there one in the apartment I haven't seen yet?" Melanie snaps playfully and pulls a face at Bryan to which his only response is an eye roll.

She gets up from the couch and walks over to him. "Oh quit it, would you!" Melanie quips from his side as he leans down to kiss her cheek. "He's only fictional. He's got nothing on you."

Looking like he could use a change of conversation, Bryan clears off the table and asks, "So how did your cake baking go?" Taking stock of the kitchen as I pull out the last of the take-out containers, it actually doesn't look half bad. Maybe Maddy's finally getting the hang of it. This was her fourth attempt, after all.

"Thanks to Betty Crocker over there," she tips her chin at Melanie, "it went fabulously!"

Maddy pulls some dishes out of the cabinet and hands them to Melanie. Plates are loaded and passed; laughs are shared and Cheerios are thrown. It's a fairly standard meal where the four of us are concerned—well, five actually. Ever since Melanie and Bryan moved in together earlier in the summer, we've become a pretty tight-knit group. They only live about thirty minutes away, so getting together once or twice a week isn't all that difficult.

There's never really a lull in the conversation. Bryan and I usually talk sports—soccer for him, baseball for me. The girls are usually engrossed in talking about whatever book they've just finished, or whatever it is that girls talk about. It's nice having Melanie and Bryan here. It makes Maddy and I feel less alone. All of the people at our jobs or at school with Maddy, who we could make friends with, and who are the same ages as us are in a completely different stage than we are.

There aren't many married couples in their early twenties and even though Melanie and Bryan aren't married, they're the closest thing we'll find. Most of the people our age are only interested in partying or getting laid.

Not that I have anything against getting laid.

By the end of the meal, Braden looks like he's about to fall asleep in his chair, so I unbuckle him before he passes out in his food. "I'm going to go put him down while you guys clean up, okay?" Melanie kisses him goodnight and goes to help Maddy with the rest of the dishes.

Maddy peers over her shoulder from the sink. "Thanks, baby."

After a quick bath, one where I got more water on me than Braden, and a fresh set of pajamas, I rock him to sleep. I'm effortlessly gliding back and forth in the rocker with my son nestled in my arms. These are the moments when I know, that no matter what's gone wrong in my life, no matter what mistakes and trials my future brings, I will at least have done one thing right.

Resting my cheek to the small tuft of light brown hair on top of his head, I tell Braden, "You're the best part of my life, little man."

"And this is the best part of mine." Maddy speaks softly from the just-cracked-open door.

Braden squirms in my arms, but quickly calms down and nuzzles back into me. Maddy sits crossed-legged on the ottoman of the glider and stares dreamily at me.

"I think you're his favorite," she whispers quietly afraid to wake him.

"Nah, he's a momma's boy through and through." I kiss his head again. "But his mom is pretty freaking amazing, so that's alright by me." I wink at her and her face beams with pride.

"Mel and Bryan leave already?" I keep my voice low, but with his cheek pressed up against my chest, he still moves slightly at the vibrations of my words.

"Yeah, they had to go put together Braden's gift for the party tomorrow." She shrugs her shoulders, but then adds, "I swear to God, if they got him a drum set, they are *so* going to get it as a hand-me-down when they have kids."

After a few more minutes of rocking, he's finally out cold, so I put him down in his crib. Maddy moves to my side, and says, "G'night, sweet boy. Sleep tight," as she pulls a light blanket over him. We tiptoe out of the room, and when we're in the hallway, I pull Maddy close to me once again.

Running my nose up the length of hers, I mumble against her lips, "I think you owe me something, Mrs. Connely."

"Oh yeah, and what would that be exactly?" she asks as she squeezes my ass, pulling our bodies together again.

"You know perfectly well what you owe me, baby." I rain kisses on her lips, across her cheek and tenderly lick that sweet spot on her neck before adding, "And I'd like to cash in on that now."

Before she even has a chance to answer me, my lips crash into hers. Nipping and softly biting at her plump lower lip causes her to groan. The opening her groan provides is all the space I need to slide my tongue into her hot mouth. Through the heated passion, I groan into her mouth, "God, Maddy. You're so fucking sweet."

We stumble into our room—arms groping, tongues licking, hearts racing. None too gently, I lower her onto the bed and revel in the feel of my body pushing hers into the mattress. Her legs wrap around my hips and pull us closer together.

"I want you." Maddy pushes up into me and grinds her hips against my cock. "Oh, God. Reid." Her voice is throaty and filled with need, and it drives me fucking crazy. My mind can't even function enough to say anything. I just want her and I don't want anything to get in the way. I lean back on my calves and unsnap her jeans. Just as she arches her hips so that I can slide them off, Braden unleashes a wailing scream from his room.

We sit quietly for a minute and hope he'll be able to calm himself, but we're not that lucky. "He's lucky he's cute," I huff as I stand from the bed. I turn around when I'm at the door and look back at Maddy. Her golden hair is splayed out like sunrays across her pillow and her chest rises and falls quickly as she works to calm her breathing. "Don't you dare move a muscle. I'll be right back." She nods as I wink at her.

The screaming is at an all-time high. Braden's face is red and streaked with tears, but when he hears me walk in the room, he quiets a little. That doesn't last long and his cries pick up in intensity. "Hey, hey, what's going on, buddy?" I try to calm him without having to rock him, but it doesn't look like that's going to happen. Standing up in his crib, he's reaching out for me. He's been crying so hard that he can't quite catch his breath. "Okay, I gotcha. Shh, shh, it's alright." Tucking him under my chin and against my chest, I sink down into the glider once again and rub his back. While the screaming has subsided, he's still uncomfortable, and more importantly, he's not asleep.

"Buddy, you gotta learn a little something about Mommy and Daddy time. This is so not cool." Braden grunts and I can't help but chuckle. It's like he actually understood me—right, like I'd be so lucky.

Gently patting his back, I try to soothe him some more. When he stretches out his legs rigidly and grunts once more, I know exactly what the problem is. With a few more pats to the back, he lets it rip and his body relaxes instantly. "Seriously, all of that screaming over a fart?" He coos and cuddles into me. I kiss the top of his head and smile. "You've seen how hot Mommy is, right? Do you hate me or something?" I joke with him even though he has no clue what I'm talking about. "Just wait, little man. I'll get you back somehow. Just you wait." He farts again as if he's trying to tell me, "Take that, Dad." Shaking my head, I laugh at him once again.

I put him back in his crib after a few minutes. Whispering softly, I tell him, "Night, buddy."

Maddy's light snoring is the only thing that greets me as I walk back into our room. Slipping out of my jeans, I mumble, "So much for that, huh?" I know she's exhausted—hell, so am I—but we've really got to break out of this once a week routine. It's killing me!

I slide under the covers and Maddy curls over to her side. Wrapped in the sheets, I spoon up behind her and fall asleep to the thoughts of a very sweet wake up call.

CHAPTER TWO

Reid

As the sun filters in the next morning, I reach to my side realize I'm alone. Great. So much for our early morning romp I was looking forward to.

It's just past six in the morning, and the apartment is wrapped in a sense of calm and quiet which only appears before Braden is awake.

Very carefully, I peek into Braden's room and see he's still sleeping. Walking out into the living room, I realize Maddy's not here. She must still be out on her morning run. Well, at least she'll definitely be awake when she gets home.

Hmm—thoughts of steamy, shower sex race around in my blue-balled brain.

Just as I start getting the coffee ready to brew, Maddy sneaks in the front door—obviously trying to be as quiet as possible so that she doesn't wake Braden. She catches sight of me in the kitchen and mimes a sleeping motion with her hands. The gesture that I want to mime about what I want to do to her will likely end in me having to sleep on the couch, so I think better of it and just nod about Braden still being asleep.

I pull down two mugs for us as Maddy walks over to the fridge to grab a bottle of water. Heat ripples off her sweat-glistened body as she moves past me. My brain is stuck in some sex-crazed, slow-motion haze and the droplet of sweat that has just beaded at her neck drifts slowly down the upper swell of her breast before plummeting rapidly into her cleavage. She'd always had a nice rack, but ever since she had the baby…yeah, really nice. Really, really nice.

And the tops of those exceptional breasts are currently popping out of her tight, hot-pink sports bra. Her chest is heaving as she works to catch her breath while chugging her water. When a rogue drop of water trickles down her chin and races behind the bead of sweat, lodged in between her soft flesh, my cock twitches to life. Of course, she catches me staring and immediately thinks the worst.

"Stop!" Maddy wraps her arm around her stomach as if doing so is going to hide something. "Why do you look at me like that?" She always seems the most self-conscious after she runs, which is ironic if you ask me. I think she looks fucking hot. She should be all high on endorphins and shit like that. But, for whatever reason, since the pregnancy changed her body, her runs became less about doing something she enjoyed and more about doing something she felt obligated to do.

I step closer to her and stare down into her bright, green eyes. Swiping a piece of hair from her forehead, I angle my head to the side. "Like what?" I question with a hint of annoyance in my voice. We've already been here before, and while I can accept her body has changed, she can't.

"Forget it. I'm not getting into *that* this morning." She chugs the last of her water. "I'm going to shower before he gets up." She huffs as she tosses her water bottle into the recycling and I'm left speechless at our exchange.

It's amazing how quickly her attitude shifts. Last night, she was all hot and bothered at the idea of me wanting her; my attraction to her was acceptable. But now, if I look at her like I want her, which apparently makes me crazy, then I'm somehow insulting her.

I mumble, "Okay," as she walks past me once again and inhale deeply. She smells like a sultry mixture of clean and dirty—citrusy shampoo and salty sweat; fresh, summer air and hot, sweaty woman.

There is no way on earth I'm letting her shower by herself, especially if she thinks it's wrong of me to be attracted to her "gross, stretched out, baby-body" as she calls it.

When I hear the water start up and the shower curtain slide closed, I quietly open the bathroom door and join her under the hot spray.

With her back to my front, she grunts—an exasperated noise—and leers over her shoulder. "What?" she huffs with an attitude that I've seen all too often—one of which I'm not too fond. Her light-blonde-turned-brown hair is splayed across her back as she lifts her face to the water. When she raises her arms to wring out her hair, I band my arms around her waist. Immediately, I feel her tense.

Resting my chin on her shoulder, I nuzzle into her slick skin and lick a path through the water sliding down her neck. "Talk to me, Maddy. Please?"

Marginally, she relaxes into my embrace. Folding her arms on top of mine, she laces our fingers together and turns to face me. "There's nothing really to talk about." She shrugs her shoulders lamely.

Turning her around in my arms, I lift her chin with my finger and gaze into her mossy-colored eyes. It's tough to tell since we're in the shower and all, but I see the shimmer of tears there. Cupping her cheeks tenderly, I silently will her to open up. When she doesn't, I have to resort to words. "There clearly is something wrong. Today is supposed to be a happy day. And here we are in a shower, not doing what we do best in showers because you're obviously upset. So talk to me, please." I lean down and kiss her forehead as she wraps her arms around my waist and leans into my body.

The feel of her tits crushing into my chest, her nipples grazing along my skin, drives me crazy. But I need for her to open up first before I can push the moment any further. Scenes from some stupid cooking show she made me watch the other day race alongside those of a ball game I watched last night and miraculously, I keep my erection at bay.

For now.

I let my fingertips skim over the peachy skin of her back and smile into her hair when I feel goose bumps dot her flesh. Maddy's shuddery sigh vibrates against my chest. "Today is a happy day, but I guess I just thought I would be in a different place. That's all. I know it's silly to let how I feel get in the way of our son's birthday, but I just...I don't...I still feel disgusting."

Laughter bubbles in my chest and she slaps my arm. "What?" There's anger in her eyes. She hates when she thinks I'm laughing at her, but she should know by now that I'm laughing at how ridiculous she's being.

"You've got to be fucking kidding me? You? Disgusting? That thought *never* crossed my mind." I hope she can hear the sincerity in my words, see the pleading in my eyes. No such luck, apparently. She just turns away from me and shuts off the water, essentially putting her foot down on the conversation we obviously need to have.

We move around the bathroom like two people who are accustomed to sharing the small space. She steps to the right and wraps herself in a towel as I move to the left to dry my hair. Her shoulders sag under the defeat of her self-consciousness as she walks across into our bedroom. I follow her and marvel at the sexy sway of her hips. The round curve of her ass dances beneath the cotton and the soft slope where her neck meets her shoulder is dotted with beads of water.

Braden is still sleeping peacefully, so I click the door closed behind me and unhook the towel from around her chest.

"Reid! Give that back!" she huffs angrily as she tries to cover up her breasts with her arms. If she thinks that's going to keep me from getting excited, then she's most definitely wrong. The sight of her creamy flesh spilling out from behind her lean arms makes my groin jump to life.

Insta-rock-hard.

I drop my towel from my waist and stand so close to her that the evidence of just how hot I think she is pokes her in the thigh. "Drop your arms," I command with a gruff voice that she doesn't listen to, of course.

"We have a lot to do today. Can we just deal with this later?" Her annoyed words float over her shoulder as she turns away from me to get some clothes from her side of the dresser.

Now, I'm pissed. I can't say I understand her insecurities—she'll always be perfect in my eyes, but I can at least recognize them and try to make them vanish.

I stand behind her and turn her around in my arms. "No, we will deal with this now." She takes a step back away from me. Whatever clothes she's just pulled out of the drawer are dropped to the floor when she hears the tone of my voice. "Oh, an eye roll. I've never seen that one before, Maddy." Yeah, that one just gets me another eye roll.

"Oh, it's on now." Waggling an eyebrow, I stalk toward her as she moves backward. When the back of her knees bump into the bed, even though she stumbles slightly, she manages to stay upright. Stepping into her space, I motion as if I'm going to kiss her, but pull back from her lips at the last second. I know she wants me, and the inch she just leaned into me, more than proves it. I move into her again, snake one arm around her waist and pull her toward me as my hand splays across her lower back. Fisting her hair at the nape of her neck with my other hand, I tilt her head to the side and unleash my tongue on her neck. Alternating between sweet licks and tender bites causes her body to melt into mine. I press my fingers firmly into the dimples of her lower back—fuck, those are sexy—and lift her slightly off the floor.

As I drop her on the bed, she gasps in shock. I lie beside her and trail my finger down the middle of her body. "Now, you're going to listen very carefully. You. Are. Beautiful." She turns her head to the side, trying to deny me my words. Cupping her chin, I turn her face back to mine. "You are. That's it. Now, let me finish." She's still all pouty, so I straddle her. Yep, *that* got her attention, real quick.

With one of my hands, I encircle both of her wrists and raise them above her head. With the other hand, I slowly tickle the soft skin of her arms. I catch her eyes roll back in her head and goose bumps race in the wake of my fingers. "Leave your arms there." She nods subtly at my command. Lips replace my fingers and I kiss every inch I can reach. When I finally make my way to her breasts, my cock twitches against her belly. She feels it and stares at me—a look of disbelief flitting across her face. "Yes," I answer her unasked question, "you do that to me."

My lips return to their previous job of bringing her to the brink of pleasure. As they lick and nip at her neck and collarbone, I gently squeeze her breasts. Strumming my thumbs over the puckered tips causes her to groan. "So responsive...so beautiful." I suck a nipple deep into my mouth while I pinch and roll the other between my finger and thumb. Her hips thrash about wildly and arch in the air searching for some kind of relief. "Soon, baby. Very soon. Just let me finish convincing you."

I rake my teeth over her hardened nipple one last time and grumble a purely male sound of satisfaction when she calls out my name. My restraint is paper-thin at this point. Whether she sees her beauty or not, I need her. I need to taste her; I need to bury myself inside of her.

In a lightning quick move, I kneel on the floor at the edge of the bed and pull her ankles so that her legs dangle over the side. Pulling a leg over each shoulder, I run the length of my nose up the inside of her thighs. The way she smells, the way she looks drives me fucking crazy.

Oh so gently, with just the lightest touch of the tip of my tongue, I lick down the center of her pussy. "More Reid, more...please." She arches her back, trying to push her wetness into my face. I tsk at her and press her hips back down to the mattress. Feeling her stiffen as I touch her belly is like taking two steps back. "I felt that. Do we need to start all over again?" I chide her playfully, but I can tell that no matter how turned on she may be, her insecurities are never far away. Kissing a seductive path up and over her mound, towards her stomach—which she obviously still hates—I let my lips linger on her belly button for a few seconds. Planting a reverent kiss there, I look up into her jade eyes. "You grew a person in here. Our baby. A tiny, little perfect boy who is half you and half me. No matter how you see it, your body is *more* perfect to me now than it ever was before. Your body gave me, gave us, the most beautiful thing in the world." I catch a flicker of emotion on her face as she lets my words register in her brain. Hoping that they're sinking in and not pissing her off, I finish what I need to tell her. "You might not think you're perfect, but I think you're flawless. Every," a soft kiss, "single," a gentle bite, "inch," a hot, wet, lick, "of you is absolutely perfect."

I don't wait to see if she accepts my declarations because I have every intention of showing her just how beautiful I find her new body. When I slide two fingers into her, I swear I hear a sigh of relief hiss through her lips. Curling them forward, I massage her relentlessly in a rhythm that has her pulsing and clenching around my fingers. Her clit pokes out from behind her glistening lips, begging me to lash it with my tongue.

Challenge accepted.

Alternating between rapid flicks and broad strokes, my tongue works its magic on her body. "Fuck…Reid…I'm close…" I see her fists clench the sheets in a white-knuckled grasp. If the vise grip her pussy has on my fingers is any indication, she's going to come hard and soon. But I need her to come around my cock. I need her to feel as connected to me as I do to her. She whimpers, actually fucking whimpers, when I pull my fingers from her pussy. I lick my fingers clean as she watches, wide-eyed, but I know it turns her on when I do this. She's told me as much.

Standing before her, with her legs still draped over the side of the bed, I pull both her ankles up to my shoulder. Kneeling in the inch of space at the edge of the mattress, I drive into her, hard and fast. Hot, wet, tight—perfect. "Fucking…Maddy…my God, baby." My hips are angled up on each thrust, and I feel her tighten around me as I hit that spot that drives her crazy. With her legs in one hand up against my chest, I reach down to tweak her nipple with the other. Her body goes limp as I feel the ripples of her orgasm against my twitching cock. It's too soon; I don't want to come yet. It takes every ounce of restraint I possess to let the tsunami of her climax pass without coming myself.

When the rapid fluttering of her pussy slows to a seductive beat, I flip her over and she balances her weight on her knees and elbows. "Your ass is a work of art." I bite it not-so-gently, and I can't repress the smile which spreads across my face when I see her skin prickle under the pressure of my teeth. She crawls more toward the middle of the bed and now I really have some leverage. Banding my arm around her waist and digging my other into her hip, I sink into her—inch by agonizing inch. I pull out slowly only to pound into her with such ferocity that her body actually goes limp in my arms.

"Maddy…" Her name comes out on a low groan as my orgasm gathers at the base of my spine and erupts with more force than is humanly possible. We collapse together on the bed—her back to my front, curled in a spoon. I sweep her hair away from her neck and plant a kiss on her shoulder. "Before you had Braden, you were the most beautiful girl I'd ever seen. And now since you've had him, you're the most stunning woman on the planet." She turns around in my arms; her lips pull up in at the corners in a shy, but beautiful way.

"Thank you for saying that, even though…"

"No," I say with finality. "There is no 'even though.' And if you need me to remind you more often, you know I'm up to the challenge." I squeeze her ass and press my groin into hers to let her know just what I mean by *reminding* her.

"Wanna remind me again later?" A quirked eyebrow and girlish smile accompany her question, and I have a feeling my plan worked at least a little.

"Absofrigginlutely."

Relaxing quietly in the haze of our morning romp, we go over everything we need to do for the day. The party is around noon at Momma's house, so if we want to get everything together and over there in time to set up, we need to get our asses in gear. When we hear Braden start babbling to himself in the next room, we get dressed and get on with our day.

CHAPTER THREE

Maddy

"Hey, birthday boy!" Momma reaches for the baby and he smiles and laughs at her silly faces. Walking into Momma's house will always feel like coming back home.

"Let me help you there, Reid." Evan walks out of the kitchen tossing a dishtowel over his shoulder.

"Thanks, Evan. Good to see you again." Reid and Evan do that guy greeting that still makes me laugh—a handshake, half hug, half back-slap kind of thing—and then they bring the bags into the kitchen where Evan is putting the finishing touches on the food.

Momma and I bring Braden into the backyard, which has been transformed into a little boy's racecar dream come true. There are balloons everywhere and the tables are covered in racing stripe tablecloths. "What do you think?"

Gasping through the hand covering my mouth, I squeal in delight. "Momma! It's perfect. Thank you so much for letting us do this here." She pulls the 'are you kidding me' face and puts Braden in his pack-n-play where a new set of toy cars waits for him. Melanie and Bryan join us in the back and help us get everything else set up. "Wow, Mom. When you go for a theme, you really kill it, huh?" Melanie whistles as she scans the yard before walking over to Braden and kissing the top of his head.

"It's an important day, so I just wanted to make sure everything was perfect." Momma winks at me before she makes her way back into the kitchen to help Evan with the rest of the food. "Bryan, can you come help me carry out some of the drinks?" Momma calls from the back door and Bryan pops a kiss to Melanie's cheek before running off to help her.

"So…" I elbow Melanie in the side, but she just shrugs her shoulders.

"So what?"

"Oh cut it! Did you talk to Bryan last night?" I elbow her again and she blushes. Bryan and Melanie just moved in together last week, and while the last few months of their relationship has been smooth sailing, to say they got off to a rough start is an understatement.

"Kinda, but not really," she responds rather shyly.

"Oh, so that's how you're going to play it, huh? Come on, spill it, girl! You got out of it last night by bringing up your newest book boyfriend, but that's not going to work now." I arch an eyebrow at her. She's not getting out of it this time.

She flops down onto the bench at the picnic table and starts picking at a non-existent piece of fuzz on her shirt. "You want the truth?" She still hasn't made eye contact with me.

"Of course I want the truth, Mel." I place my hand on top of hers and squeeze gently. "Is something going on?"

"No, nothing's going on...it's just, I guess it's not as easy as we thought, and that's not exactly an easy conversation to bring up, you know."

"Do you want to talk about it?" I know how closed-up Melanie can get and I hate what it did to her last time her world was in upheaval. So even if she tells me she doesn't want to talk, I'll get it out of her.

But, much to my surprise, she actually opens up. "Things between Bryan and I are great, actually. It's just weird to be so settled down and be so young. I know Bryan loves me and I love him, but we're only in our early twenties. I guess sometimes I get a little freaked out thinking about how young we are that's all." I'm so proud of her for finally being able to open up about what she's afraid of, that I can't help but smile at her.

"Does it help to know I feel the same way about me and Reid?" Melanie turns her head to me so quickly that she almost falls off the bench.

"But you guys are married and have a kid together."

"I know, Mel, and I really do love our life, but I can't say it's not scary to think about how young we are. But you know what? At the end of the day, I know I'm happy. If I can end each day feeling happy about the life we've created, then who cares how old I am."

"I know you're right, Maddy. I am deliriously happy with Bryan; I just hope he's happy with me."

She huffs at me when I shoot her my best 'you're out of your freaking mind' face. "He wouldn't be inside with your mom helping and spending the day with your family if he wasn't crazy in love with you."

"You don't get it, Maddy. You're perfect through and through. Reid will never look at another woman the way he looks at you. I still feel less than perfect some days and I hate that I let those feelings seep into my relationship." Reid's words from earlier this morning flash through my brain and I instantly feel the weight of his love, settling deep in my chest, alleviating some of my perceived imperfections.

"I get it more than you think, Mel." Without getting into the sexier details of my morning, I share with her just how uncomfortable I feel about my post baby-body. Being able to talk to another girl about body issues somehow helps me feel much better about them. We're able to boost each other up without bringing each other down. We joke about grandma arm-flab, Freddy Kruger-like stretch marks, and junk in the trunk. Somehow, by the end of our chat, we've exorcised some of our demons—ones that we see in a much worse light than anyone else ever would.

By the time everyone else comes back outside, we've moved on to laughing about the shortcomings of our significant others. "I know seriously, how difficult is it to drop the dirty clothes *in* the laundry basket instead of *next* to it."

"Pfft. That's nothing. Reid dutch-ovened me the other night. I seriously thought I was going to throw up." I make a mock-gagging noise, which Braden finds hilarious. He starts making farting noises with his tongue, which only adds to our laughter.

"Oh my God, the farting. Seriously, I had no clue guys farted that much." Melanie laughs hysterically just as Bryan and Reid walk up behind us.

"You better watch it there, Maddy. You're no better." Reid pulls a face at me as he lifts Braden up into the sky. "Little man here takes after you in more than just being cute, you know."

"Yeah, well at least I don't suffocate you under the sheets! And for the record, girls do not stink nearly as bad as boys." Sticking my tongue out at him only adds to the childishness of this exchange. When Reid looks over to Bryan to weigh in, he pretends to be busy not hearing a word Reid just said.

"So you're just going to leave me hanging like that?"

"Um, yeah, I am." Pulling Melanie to his side, he smiles wide. "I sleep with her. I'm not that dumb." We all get lost in a fit of giggles joking around with each other. In the midst of it all, Melanie and I share a look of understanding, of sisterhood. In that split second of eye contact, we know we'll both be okay—all four of us will be okay. Despite our insecurities about our bodies, and our concerns about our age, the four of us seem to share something that can never be taken away from us.

The bonds of being a family.

The rest of the afternoon passes in more laughter and happy conversations. For the most part, the guys man the grill. Men and their meat—don't even get me started. As I watch Reid try to put out a burger that has somehow caught on fire, Dylan struts up beside me. "Hey! I was wondering when you were going to get here." He hugs me and pops a quick kiss on the top of my head before reaching for Braden.

"Hey, little man. Happy birthday." Dylan tosses him in the air a few times to which Braden's reaction is giggles. Mine is to stop breathing. Seriously, why do people feel the need to toss my baby into the air?

Reid comes up behind Dylan and claps him on the shoulder. "Hey, man. Good to see you."

As if it's written into their DNA, Reid and Dylan immediately start talking about some baseball game that went into forty extra innings or something like that. I just tune them out and greet the rest of the guests as they arrive.

After dinner is done and it's time to serve the cake, I go into the kitchen to get out my masterpiece. Okay, fine. It's so not a masterpiece, but when I put the "1" birthday candle into the center of the best racecar-shaped cake I'll ever make, I get a little emotional.

Reid surprises me as he wraps his arms around my waist from behind. "It turned out great, babe."

"Ehh, it's not perfect, but I'm glad I was finally able to come up with something."

"It's chocolate and icing—that's all a one-year-old needs." He kisses my temple and carries the cake out to Braden who's strapped into his high chair out on the back deck.

Reid and I stand next to Braden who looks more than shell-shocked when everyone starts singing. But at the end of the song, when everyone starts clapping, Braden brings his chubby little hands together and claps along with them. He just stares at his cake for a minute, like he doesn't know what to do. Leave it to Reid to show him, though.

"Like this, B," he says as he swipes his finger through the icing and right onto my cheek. I watch Reid lick the icing from his finger, more than a little shocked he just cake-faced me. Going in for the kill, I grab a handful of cake and toss it at him. Agile as ever, he ducks and it lands in Melanie's hair.

She grabs a cupcake from the table next to her and launches it me. When it hits me square in the chest, Momma calls out, "Stop…" But before she can get any more words out, Evan squishes a cupcake on the top of her head. She turns quickly on her heels and shoots Evan a death stare quickly followed by a fit of laughter. "Oh, that's it, Ev!" she calls out as she smashes a cupcake into his cheek. Reid's busy watching the food-fight he just started. Catching him off-guard, I manage to smear a handful of cake into his face. He quickly repays the favor while managing to leave a streak of icing across my chest.

Through it all, Braden catches on, and by the time we look over at him, he's covered in icing from ear-to-ear. Everyone "ohhs" and "ahhs" at how cute he's being when he licks his fingers and says, "Mmmm."

Calling a truce, Reid and I stand next to Braden and each kiss a cheek—another perfect snapshot to add to our growing list of happy memories.

When most of the chaos of our little food-fight calms, Momma takes Braden inside to wash him up. Reid hands me a napkin and leans into my ear. With a seductive lilt to his voice, he whispers, "Can I lick you clean?"

"Maybe. Under one condition, though?" His eyes widen a little and I know he must be recalling what we did only hours ago.

"Anything, you name it," he mumbles his words against my ear and chills race across my skin.

"No more dutch ovens." Reid taps his frosting-covered lower lip as if he's actually weighing his options, before he plants a slow, sweet kiss to my lips.

"I think that can be arranged."

He grins at me goofily, but when I pull his ear down to my lips and whisper, "Good, then you can lick me all you want." His smile is replaced by a look of surprise.

Leaving him standing there, slack-jawed and shocked, I sit with Braden, who is now somewhat clean, so that he can open his presents. Of course, he finds the wrapping paper more entertaining than the toys themselves.

After everyone leaves and all of the gifts and leftovers are packed in the Jeep, we say our goodbyes and head home. Braden falls asleep on the ride home and Reid and I get lost in sharing some of our happiest, and funniest, memories of the past year.

Once everything is unloaded and Braden is in his crib, I turn on the shower and call out to Reid who is sitting on the couch in the living room.

"Wanna join me?" I make a "come hither" motion with my finger as I crack the door opened just enough for him to catch a glimpse of me naked. If he was less coordinated, he might have tripped over his own two feet as he launched himself from the couch to race toward me.

It's a perfect way to bookend a perfect day.

Fall
Late October 2014

CHAPTER FOUR

Reid

"You think you could actually hit the ball out of the infield this time?" I toss Bryan a bat as he shoots me the "shut the fuck up" face.

"Would you leave him alone?" Dylan, the team captain and always the diplomat, claps Bryan on the shoulder. "Reid once broke his nose because the ball he'd just bunted bounced off the plate and popped him right in the face." Of course, Dylan and Bryan share a laugh at my expense, but that was actually pretty funny. Except for the shit-storm I caught from my father about not being in proper form and how I could have won the game for my team if I knew what the fuck I was doing.

Nothing like a little encouragement from your old man, huh?

When the umpire calls "batter up," Bryan takes one last practice swing. Leaning up against the fence, Dylan coaches Bryan through his at-bat and he actually manages to get a base hit. All kidding aside, Dylan's a great coach.

"Thanks for letting him join." I hold up one finger to Bryan to remind him there's only one out. Without turning around, I angle my head to the bleachers behind us where Maddy and Melanie are cheering us on. "It means a lot to the girls, and to me."

"Anytime, man. Besides we needed an extra player otherwise the team would have had to forfeit the season." The Bridge, where Dylan and I work as Gay-Straight Alliance advocates, has always put up a company softball team in the local fall-ball league. I played last year and I can't even begin to explain the memories that came to the surface. Being on the field again with Dylan, made me miss Shane so much that there were some days I thought of quitting. But when Maddy reminded me that Shane would be happier with me being on the field than at home angry over him being gone, I knew that I had to stay.

The batter after Bryan manages a single and Bryan squeezes an extra base off a throwing error. With only one out and our strongest player at bat, Todd, who is pretty much two-hundred-and-fifty-pounds of solid muscle, our chances of winning this game, and the league championship, are fairly decent.

Just as expected, Todd lifts a fly ball into left field. Bryan watches it soar overhead and starts running for home. The left-fielder is crazy fast and before Bryan even realizes it, he is in position to catch the ball; he's just standing out there waiting for it to drop in his glove. Dylan and I are flailing our arms and yelling, "Go back! Go back!" He's still not familiar with all of the rules of the game, so Bryan stops in the middle of the baseline and just stares at us with a dumbfounded look on his face. "Dude, go back!" I call out one last time before he seems to recall his running error.

Who the hell could have predicted what happens next, but all of a sudden, the left-fielder trips over his own feet or a large rock or something like that, and the ball drops to the ground next to him. Dylan and I resume yelling for Bryan to run. Confusion sets in on Bryan who hasn't yet figured out the ball was not caught. Behind me, I hear Melanie screaming for Bryan to slide as the center fielder, who was backing up the play, launches the ball towards home plate. Clapping, yelling, screaming, general chaos ensues as both Bryan and the ball arrive at home plate at the same time. The softball gods must be on our side today, because by some miracle, Bryan slides his foot around the catcher and somehow completely avoids the tag.

"Safe!" The umpire yells out as he slashes his arms through the air. Bryan jumps up from his slide only to be tackled to the ground by the rest of the team. Before he even sees it coming, one of the guys has the water cooler hoisted up over his shoulder, ready to dump it on Bryan's head.

"Ah, fuck! That's cold!"

"Better you than me," I laugh as I hand him his hat that got lost in the pile up after the play at the plate.

"Way to go, Bry!" Dylan high fives Bryan and the rest of the team follows. The umpire hands us our championship plaque and we line up quickly to take a picture for the office. It's our third year in a row as league champions and it's fair to say that Bryan has won himself a spot on the team from here on out.

After the picture is taken and most of the guys head out to their cars, Dylan, Bryan and I grab the last of the gear. "Great game, guys." Maddy and Melanie come over to us as we're packing up the last of our things. Braden is sitting up in his stroller playing with some of his toys. Reaching up on her toes, Maddy plants a quick kiss on my cheek and surprises me more than a little when she slaps my ass.

"No thanks to Bryan's superb base running skills," Dylan jokingly punches him on the arm.

"Whatever." He chugs down his water as Melanie wraps her arm around his waist.

"I thought you were great!" I know Melanie means well, but publicly defending your boyfriend's non-existent softball skills is only going to make him the butt of more of our jokes.

We all walk out to the parking lot as a group. "You guys want to grab a beer down at Murray's?" Dylan asks over the hood of his car. A few of our other teammates decided to head home, needing to ice and rest before work tomorrow morning, but Todd and a couple other guys are heading to the bar. Bryan and I look at Maddy and Melanie seeking approval without really wanting to ask for it—yeah, I guess you could say we're a little whipped.

Whatever, I enjoy sex and I fully intend to get some tonight. So pissing Maddy off isn't exactly on my radar. Besides, I know that when Dylan asks to head out for a few drinks, he really needs to talk.

I can't ever say 'no' to him when he needs to get something off his chest.

Answering our silent question, Maddy grabs the keys to the Jeep. "Yeah, go have fun. We'll see you guys in a bit." I help her get Braden is his seat and toss Bryan a dry shirt from my gym bag.

"I promise I won't be late." As I lean through the window and kiss her goodbye, she mumbles against my lips, "You better not be." She winks at me seductively before her and Melanie pull away.

We each grab a stool at the bar and order a Bud while mindlessly zoning out to ESPN. There isn't much to guys' conversation on a Sunday afternoon in a bar. Really, the main reason we go is to get away from talking. There's something so very relaxing about just being out with the guys watching a game on TV—any game, really—and not having to say a word.

About an hour after we arrive, Bryan finishes the last of his one and only beer. "I'm out, guys." He slides his stool forward. "I'm going to catch a ride with Todd. I've got class in the morning and so does Melanie. I'll see you next weekend, yeah?"

"Sure thing, man. Great job today," Dylan calls out over his shoulder without really taking his eyes off the screen above the bar.

The bar erupts into loud screams and cheers as the playoff game ends in a walk-off homerun. Dylan orders another drink, and when the volume level returns to normal, he clears his throat.

"So, I got a call in the office on Friday." The quiet and unsure quality of his voice immediately sets me on edge. I twist in my seat to face him and silently prompt him to continue.

"It was on the support line and the caller didn't give a name, but I swear I knew who it was." He takes a swig of his beer as he seems to mentally flip through the hundreds of students we've met since the school year started in September.

"Dylan, there's no way you could know. We visit at least two schools a week and it's been what, like five weeks now since we started our fall assemblies?"

Scrubbing his hand over his face, he puffs out a deep, frustrated breath. "Yeah, I know. But when I heard her voice on the line, it just sounded so familiar. She was so sad. I could hear her pain. I could tell she was crying, but before I could get her to say much of anything, she hung up."

"Maybe it'll come to you." I finish off the last of my beer and slide my glass over to the bartender.

Dylan's eyebrows are furrowed together and he looks like he's scanning the bar top to try and read something written there in invisible ink. "I think...I mean, I could be making this up, but I think before she said she was an anonymous caller, it sounded like her name was on the tip of her tongue."

"Did she say anything else that would give you some kind of clue? A friend's name or something like that?"

I can tell he's mentally replaying the conversation, so when the light bulb goes off over his head, I grin and wait for him to share.

"She said 'Cane would kill me if he knew I was calling.' After that, I couldn't make out anything because she was sobbing so badly. Then, the line went dead."

"Cane? You sure?" I need to double check, make sure my ears aren't playing tricks on me.

"Yeah, I'm certain because I remember thinking I wish she'd give me her name too so that I could put it all together and go help her out some more."

"There was a kid in my group last week at Lincoln Memorial whose name was Cane. It can't be all that common of a name, can it?" I clearly remember the kid too. Tall and skinny, dressed in a punk-rock inspired wardrobe from head to toe. He stayed after the assembly when I held a voluntary group session. Kids rarely open up much during those, but not Cane. He was angry and clearly hurting. I did my best to try to talk him through his pain, to get him to open up, but when he saw the other kids sitting there wide-eyed and shocked, he shut his mouth and practically stormed out of the room.

"Why don't we talk to everyone who helps with the support line to keep their eyes out for the number that called on Friday, or anything within the same area code? If any of the callers mention anything about Lincoln Memorial, then maybe we can get in touch with the principal and go back into the school." I offer up a lame smile hoping that it will help calm his racing brain, but I know it won't. Dylan cares about the kids we meet more than anyone I know. He really takes their issues to heart.

"Yeah, man. Sounds good." He stands and throws a twenty down on the bar. We walk out to his car, and for the ten minute drive to my apartment, there's an uneasy silence settling around us. I unclip my seatbelt. "Don't worry, okay. We'll figure something out." He nods but stares out the windshield, a distracted look plastered to his face. After I close the door, I pop my head back through the window. "See you tomorrow." My words almost startle him and he looks over at me as if he's seeing me for the first time since we left the bar.

I stand in the parking lot and watch him pull away. I don't want to imagine the thoughts going through his head right now. I'm sure they're about Shane. For a guy who seems to have it all together most days, he's still reeling inside. I can't force him to open up, though. The best I can do is wait for him to want to talk.

Maybe someday.

CHAPTER FIVE

Maddy

I swear I only hear every other word out of my professor's mouth. Presidents and Senators. Executive and legislative branches. I have busted my ass to get to where I am, and if I didn't need this politics course in order to graduate from my two-year program in the spring, well, then I would *so* be dropping it.

"Any questions?" he calls out dryly and he wipes his chalk-covered hands down the front of his dark brown corduroys.

Please, nobody have a question. Pretty please. I just want to go home.

Thankfully, no one asks anything. When he says, "Class dismissed," the only noise that fills the room is the sound of everyone closing up their textbooks and packing up their backpacks.

Class is over at 8:30 pm, so as long as I walk out with a group of people, I feel safe trekking through the rather poorly lit parking lot. Christina, the quiet and mousy girl who sits next to me, walks with me to my car. "I'm only a few down." She angles her head down the line of parked cars where her lights flash and her alarm chirps. "I'll get coffee next week. Large, hazelnut, with skim milk, right?" Her eyes squint together as she recalls my order from the last time she bought the coffee.

"Perfect. Thanks, Chrissy." She walks toward her car and waves. "See you next week."

I don't particularly like having to take night classes, but since I have to work during the day time, there really isn't much choice. I've taken every weekend and off-session class that the local school offers. I decided early on I wanted to double major in business and early childhood development. I eventually want to run my own day care center, and with each class I cross off my list, the more excited I grow at the possibilities that wait for me.

The drive back home passes in a blur. In short, Fridays suck. Nothing screams get me the freak home like an eight-hour workday, followed by a three-hour class that you didn't want to take in the first place. Yeah, that about sums up my day. So as the gate to my complex comes into view, it's almost as if I can feel the weight of the day—and the week for that matter—lifting from my shoulders.

I never really thought of it until we moved in here together, but I can't even begin to tell you how important it is to come home to a turned-on porch light. The dim light from the front window, adding to the soft glow of the flickering porch light, lets me know that Reid is waiting up for me, as usual.

"Hey, hun," I call out from the front door. "The baby asleep already?"

Reid peeks around the corner of the kitchen into the living room. With a rather mischievous grin on his face, he winks at me. "Nope." His face disappears behind the corner again.

Okay, cryptic much.

Stepping into the kitchen and dining room combo, I now understand what the goofy smile was all about. He's got a romantic, candle-lit dinner for two all set up. Unable to hide the shock in my voice, or on my face, Reid just laughs at me as he hands me a glass of wine.

"You cooked?"

He kisses my cheek quickly. "Don't sound so surprised. It'd be more impressive if *you* cooked." He pulls a face at me and I roll my eyes—our usual M.O. for mocking one another. "But, no I didn't cook, this time. I dropped Braden off at Momma's for a sleepover and she cooked. I did at least plan the night, so do I get some credit for that?"

I lean my head on his shoulder as he pulls me to his side. "Of course you do, babe. This is perfect." He kisses the top of my head and then moves to pull out a chair for me.

"Here, sit." As he busies himself with finishing our plates, I enjoy my glass of wine and let the day melt away. Seriously, nothing can beat a quiet, home-cooked meal with my man at the end of a crazy-ass week. Watching him move around the kitchen with such finesse and grace isn't so bad either.

He puts my plate in front of me and slides into the seat at my side. "So, how was your day?" Reid asks as he digs into the crust of Momma's world famous chicken potpie. Okay, fine. It's not *world* famous, but it's damn good.

"It was okay." I tell him about the updates to the computer system at work and how they're really not all bad, despite how much some people are still bitching about them. I seriously think that some people just enjoy complaining. "And then class was…umm, let's go with mind-numbingly boring." We share a laugh over it. He knows that politics is my least favorite class ever.

Speaking around a mouthful of food, I ask him about his day. There's an awkward pause for a second as he puts down his fork and wipes his mouth with his napkin. "I guess you could say it was interesting." His tone has me a bit wary. Interesting in his line of work could range from a high school girl hitting on him— don't laugh; it's happened before—to a scared and lonely teenager doing harm to himself. The concerned look on his face, as he scrubs his hand over his stubbled jawline, tells me that it's the latter that's bothering him.

I put my hand on top of his and lightly stroke my thumb over his wrist. "What happened? Was it about the call you and Dylan have been working on?"

"Yeah, we got another call from the girl this morning. She mentioned the same name as the last call—Cane. But, she wouldn't identify herself. We called the school and set up a meeting with the principal this afternoon to see if he might know who would be calling or why someone would mention Cane's name."

"Did he tell you anything? I mean, does the principal know who the girl is who keeps calling?"

"He didn't say anything, but I got the feeling he was hiding something." Reid takes a chug of his water before adding, "Dylan thinks the same thing. We just can't figure out what it is he's not telling us. Even when we asked the principal if the kid had any close female friends who would know him enough to call in about him, he just shrugged his shoulder. Turns out Cane is kind of a loner. The principal says he rarely sees him with anyone, actually."

"I'm sorry, Reid. I wish you could have found out at least something. Maybe the girl will call back," I add hopefully, as he stands to clear the table.

"On the one hand, I hope she does. I want to figure out who she is, but on the other hand, I hope that things—whatever things are going on that she can't talk about yet—don't get so bad that she *has* to continue calling." Though he shrugs his shoulders, I know he's got anything but "whatever" feelings about it.

I watch him as he stands in front of the sink cleaning the few dishes that we dirtied. Watching the flex and pull of his broad shoulders under the thin cotton of his t-shirt, makes my insides go warm. I stand behind him and wrap my arms around his narrow waist. Hooking my thumbs into the belt-loops of his jeans, I press my cheek up against the solid warmth of his back.

Trying to lighten the mood, I laugh as I ask, "So you didn't get asked to prom this time, huh?" I feel his chest vibrate as he chuckles. Some overly flirty senior actually did ask him to prom this past June when he was at her school for an end-of-the-year workshop. He tried to let her down easy; not wanting to assault her ego; he said he was happily married. She openly scoffed his rejection by popping her hip and squeezing her boobs together as she told him that it was his loss. "Nah, no prom dates. A few whistles and stares though." He laughs some more and he turns and pulls me to his chest.

I poke him playfully in the ribs. "Well, that's good. I wouldn't want you to think you were losing your touch or anything like that."

"First of all, they're high school girls, so um thanks but no thanks. And most importantly," he gently brushes his lips across mine in a move so sensual that I can't help but press my body into his, "I've already got the most beautiful woman in the world."

I let my hands roam across his back, before not-so-gently, grasping his perfect ass. With lips quirked in a seductive smile, I squeeze him once more to punctuate my words. "Damn straight you do. Now, take me to bed."

Without warning, he bends down and tucks his arm under my knees. I loop my arms around his neck gasping in surprise. "With pleasure, my love," he mumbles against my neck as he whisks me down the hall into our room.

After gently placing my feet on the floor, he stares intently into my eyes. He speaks no words, but his face could recite poetry. Thumbs softly brush across my cheekbones while he cups my jawline with such tenderness that leaning into his touch is instinctual. Without breaking his intense stare, he glides my top over my head. With quick fingers, my bra is unclasped and dangling before me. My skin chills in the cool air and my nipples pebble under the lusty look in Reid's eyes.

When I reach for him—to rip his shirt off, to push his jeans to the floor—he cages my small wrist in his strong grasp. "Shhh. Wait," he hushes as he finishes undressing me. I kick my jeans to the side and watch in utter amazement as he pulls his T-shirt up from behind. His body is my weakness; I tremble at the mere sight of his muscles rippling and flexing with his deliberate movements. In one swift move, he strips himself of his jeans and boxers. My mouth waters ravenously. My pulse races quickly. My insides tighten deliciously.

Reid takes me by surprise when he picks me up once more. Afraid to lose my balance, I wrap my legs around his waist. His deep blue eyes are burning with passion. I lean forward to kiss him needing to feel his lips against mine. I'm more than a little angry when he pulls back and shakes his head. "I want to take my time with you, go slow. There's no rush. I'm going to kiss every inch of your body. Run my tongue along every line and curve. I'm going to bring you to the edge of your control, just to ease you back. Drive you crazy." He plants a heated kiss to each corner of my mouth before pressing his full lips flush against mine. He licks, nips and tugs on my lower lip. When his tongue slides into my mouth, I lose hold on my control. I kiss him back with as much passion and love as I can muster.

Our mingled breath is hot and heavy. His exhales become my inhales. As if we weren't already, we become even more entwined with one another. He overwhelms every single one of my senses. His purely masculine scent—clean and earthy with just a hint of soap and cologne; his uniquely Reid taste—lust mixed with desire pushes me over the edge. The feel of his muscles bunching under my fingertips spurs on my desire to run my hands over every single centimeter of flawless male beauty holding me up.

As if he can tell that I need more of him, he lowers us to the bed. The feel of his erection pressing firmly into my stomach makes me crave him even more. I arch my back and press my hips up into his, searching for some kind of release from the beautiful torment his lips and tongue are unleashing on my breasts. As he wraps his mouth around my hardened nipple, a low moan escapes from mine. Lacing my fingers through his silky hair, I hold his head in place. He alternates between hard sucks and gentle nips until my sensitive skin is on fire. "Reid...please..."

"I know, baby. I know." He swipes his thumb across my lower lip and I lick it seductively. His eyes widen as I wrap my fingers around his wrist. Pulling his finger into my mouth, I suck and lick. Grazing my teeth over it forces a hiss of air to pass through his lips. I push his hand away from my face down to where I want it to go.

"Use your hands, please. I need to feel you touch me." The erotic groan of my words is accentuated by the rhythmic gyrating of my hips. Reid grips my hip with one hand, stilling my movements. His other hand hovers about my mound and I'm arching, stretching, reaching for him to touch me. But, the further I reach, the harder he holds me in place.

"Stay still, Maddy," he commands in his sexy-as-fuck voice that I'll never be able to ignore.

I relax back into the mattress and he releases my hip. Using the same finger that was just in my mouth, he traces a feather-light path right down the center of my wet and glistening pussy. Back and forth, back and forth. Stoking the flame that he's ignited, he's touching me everywhere but where I want him. Slow, methodical, torturous, but oh-so incredible. I close my eyes and just enjoy the feel of his fingers gliding over me.

The bed shifts as he settles in between my legs. I feel his hot breath on my thighs right before he trails soft kisses along my sensitive skin. His tongue replaces his fingers and continues along the same hot path. "Fuck, Maddy. You're drenched." He laps at my core and presses his lips briefly to my clit. "God, you taste fucking amazing." His sounds of appreciation are lost as his mouth fuses to my body. His fingers plunge into me, rubbing deep inside. Every fiber of my body belongs to him, and with a few rapid flicks of his tongue, perfectly timed with a tweaked nipple, I crash and burn beautifully under the pleasure that only Reid can deliver.

"Watching you writhe on the bed, tasting you come in my mouth, is simply the most beautiful thing in the world." He hovers above me, his lips glistening with my orgasm. I wrap my hands around his neck and pull his face to mine. Plunging my tongue into his mouth makes his cock twitch in between us. A gasp of pleasure passes between us when I feel a drop of his moisture drip onto my skin.

Wrapping my legs around his waist, I grab his ass and pull him as close to me as possible. The tip of his cock nudges at my entrance and I press forward wanting him inside of me already. He gives me an inch, but it's not enough. "More. Now. Please." My breathless words are offered up like a prayer.

"No." He leans his elbows down and places one on each side of my head, supporting his weight. "I told you. I want to go slow and savor you." He chews on his lower lip and I can tell that he's having a hard time holding back. But the fiery look in his ocean blue eyes forces me to submit to his pace.

He pushes into me, one rigid inch at a time. I revel in the feel of the bulged veins and silky skin of his cock as he slides in and out of me. "Look at me, Maddy. Look at me, now." My gaze meets his as his lips crash into mine. He wraps his arm around my waist and lifts my body up as he drives into me. His pace increases a little, but the angle—oh God, the change in the angle makes my insides pulse around him. "Come, beautiful. Come for me," he mumbles against my puckered nipple. The tenderness with which he nuzzles against my breast makes thrill bumps dot my flesh, and when his tongue streaks hotly against the hardened tip, my pussy flutters wildly around his cock.

He pushes harder and faster through my orgasm, never letting me fall completely. My body splinters into a thousand tiny pieces, but he's right there, holding me tightly to his solid chest, to put me back together again. With his face buried into the crook of my neck, his lips dance on my skin. The stubble on his jaw scrapes the top curve of my breasts. His hands roam at the softness of my waist pulling me closer as he pushes deeper.

He leans his forehead against mine as he stills his movements. His ragged breaths sweep across my face and he closes his eyes slowly. "What is it, baby? Are you okay?" I brush a lock of hair from his eyes.

"Of course I'm okay. I'm inside of you. What the hell could be wrong?" He drives into me as deep as he can and stops his movements yet again. "I just wanted to feel you pulse around me before I lose myself to you."

On his last word, he begins moving again, the sole purpose to bring us both over the edge this time. His arms band around my body as we roll on our side. Our bodies twist and tangle, push and pull, rise and fall. "Maddy...fuck..." he groans into my mouth as his tongue dances with mine. "Baby..." I call out as another wave washes over me. I scour my nails over his back as he calls my name out on one last powerful thrust.

We lay together, limbs tangled, breaths ragged, long enough for me to start drifting to sleep. His soft lips press to my forehead as he pulls me to his chest.

"You're amazing." He traces circles on my shoulders and back.

"Hmmm."

"That's all you can manage, huh?" I feel his chest vibrate under my cheek with his laughter.

"Hmmm." I can feel his heart thumping wildly under my hand.

He pops a kiss to the top of my head. "Sleep, baby. I'll let you brag about my amazingness when you wake up."

"Hmmm."

Winter
Late December 2014

CHAPTER SIX

Reid

"Alright, man. I'm out for the night." Dylan leans over the wall of my cubicle. "Wanna grab a drink before heading home? It's Friday, so you know there's a happy hour somewhere."

"Thanks, but I can't, Dyl." I power down my computer and start packing up my things. "I need to get a few last minute Christmas gifts before Maddy gets home from class tonight. Rain check?"

"Sure thing." He nods to make it seem like he's really okay with it, but I know he's not. We got another call today from our mystery girl and it's really starting to affect him that he can't figure it out.

"Hey, Dylan! Wait up. I'll walk out with you." I jog to him as he holds the elevator doors open for me. "You okay, man?" I ask as the doors ping closed.

"Yeah, I guess. Just really shaken up about these calls, that's all." Dylan shrugs his shoulders but I know deep down he's never going to be able to rid himself of the uncertainty of the situation. Knowing that it's more than Cane and this mystery caller weighing on his mind, that it's more about his guilt over not being able to save Shane, has me in knots. I hate seeing him like this and he has to learn how to forgive himself or he's never going to be able to move on.

Exiting the building, an icy blast of winter air whips across our faces. "Fuck, it's cold!" I snap my jacket closed and pull my leather gloves out of my pockets. We walk to our cars in frigid silence, partly quieted by the weather, partly by the guilt that is consuming us both.

Ours are the only cars in the lot. "Where's the Jeep?" he asks through chattering teeth.

"This beat up piece of shit," I tip my chin in the direction of Maddy's ancient Civic, "needed an oil change today. I took care of it at lunch and Maddy took the Jeep for the day."

"Still can't get her to give in on the new car thing, huh?" Dylan chuckles and tucks his hands in his pockets.

"Well, she's not going to have much of a choice after Christmas."

"You are such an over-the-top bastard, you know that?" He rolls his eyes and tosses his bag onto the passenger's seat. A tense silence descends on us. There's so much I want to say to him, but standing next to his car, in the icy winter air, I can't string the words together.

I want to yell and scream at him that it's not his fault for what happened to Shane, for what's happening now with this girl who keeps calling the hotline. But I know it's pointless. He won't listen. So, I offer up the best solution I can come up with in the few minutes that I've had to think about it.

"Listen, it's Christmas break for the schools. Why don't you take a week off from thinking about it and we'll re-group after the holidays. We can get back in touch with the principal and everything, okay?"

"Sounds good, Reid. See you in a few days." The engine turns over and roars to life. Dylan pulls away and I know that the last thing he'll be able to do is shut off his concern for the next week.

Another freezing gust blows over me as I hurry to my car. Sliding inside, I toss my bag next to me and blast the heat. The interior smells like Maddy's perfume and the heat amplifies the scent. Maybe holding onto this car isn't such a bad idea, after all. We have had a few good romps in here and I would hate to get rid of those memories.

Before I can get too distracted thinking about all of that, my phone vibrates in my pocket pulling me out of my sexy daydreams. A picture of a smiling Maddy and Braden lights up in the background and I realize I have five missed calls from her.

Swiping across the bottom of the screen with my thumb, I answer the call. "Hey, babe. What's up?"

Initially, there's just silence punctuated only by her sniffles. "Maddy, what the hell is going on?" Abruptly, I slide the shifter into drive needing to get to wherever she is. When the car fishtails in the icy parking lot, I take a deep breath and try to calm my nerves.

She still hasn't said anything and I'm about to freak the fuck out. "Maddy, where are you? Why are you crying?"

"I'm at school. Come get me. I need you to come here, now." Before I can say anything in response, she hangs up leaving me more than a little confused and extremely worried.

I try calling her back at least ten times in the ten-minute ride to the college campus, but she doesn't pick up. Spurred on by anxiety and fear, I fly into the lot and spot my Jeep parked on the far end. The Civic screeches to a stop next to the Jeep and I see someone in the passenger's seat.

My feet slip on the icy pavement as I race around to the driver's side where Maddy is sitting. Maddy lowers the window and I slip my head inside the cabin. "Reid, this is Lizzy." Maddy reaches over to the passenger and gently squeezes the girl's arm. Her small face is hidden in the shadows, but even in the darkness, she looks vaguely familiar. Angling her head more toward the light, Lizzy's features come into view.

I recognize her instantly.

She's a student from Lincoln Memorial.

"You've been calling us." It's a statement, not a question. Disbelief laces through my words. "But how did you…I mean, why are you here?" I sweep my arm to the side indicating "here" as the campus parking lot.

I look at Maddy with what I'm sure is my "what the fuck" face because she smirks knowingly at me as she steps out of the Jeep. Maddy kisses my cheek and pulls her bag over her shoulder. "She followed the Jeep after school. She thought you were driving. I'll let her explain the rest." She hugs me tightly and the sweet smell of her hair swirls in my head. "I'll see you after class, but talk to her." With one last quick kiss, Maddy turns on her heels and walks toward the building where her class takes place.

I inhale the cold night air deeply. My lungs protest as the chill seizes them, but I need a minute to gain my composure. I huff out one last cleansing breath and watch the steam from my exhale curl into the night sky.

Slicing through the uncomfortable silence, the door lets out a loud creak as I open it. I twist in my seat and face Lizzy. She's got a wad of tissues bunched up in her lap and I can see the tracks of the tears that she's been crying streak down her cheeks. Whatever it is we need to talk about can't be said in the darkness. I reach up and turn the overhead light on and I'm shocked to see that her face is all beaten and bloody.

"My God. Lizzy, what happened?" I don't even let her answer as I reach into my pocket to call the police.

Her icy-cold hand stops my dialing. "No. Please. Wait. Just let me explain." Through her wobbly and unsteady voice, I can hear determination and strength. I put my phone away and hand her another tissue from the box sitting in between us.

"Okay. Talk to me then. Is this about Cane?" I've put on my best counselor voice, but I'm sure that she can hear the fear there.

At simply mentioning his name, Lizzy recoils in her seat. She ghosts her fingers over her split lip and my gut churns in disgust. "Did he hurt you, Lizzy?"

"No!" she barks out. "No, he would never…it wasn't him…it was…oh God, I don't even know where he is. He just left." Sobs wrack her tiny body and I can no longer make any sense of her words as she muffles them into her pile of tissues.

"Shhh…it's okay. Just calm down and tell me exactly what happened." I try to keep my voice steady and relaxed, even though I'm feeling the exact opposite.

After a few moments of awkward silence, her crying slows and she regains her self-control. "Cane is my best-friend. We've know each other since kindergarten." She pauses for a minute to blow her nose—loud and not at all sounding delicate. When her breathing is steady, she continues her story, "He asked to borrow my glue stick, and when I wouldn't give it to him, we ended up wrestling over it. We had to stay inside at recess for detention and I guess we hit it off because we've been inseparable ever since." A cute, little smile curls at her lips as she retells her childhood memories.

I don't want to interrupt her, so I bite my tongue stifling the long list of questions that I want to ask. Giving her the space she needs to piece her story together, I don't say anything.

"We dated when we were in ninth grade. But really, it was the same thing as being friends. We played video games and skateboarded and all that stuff. One day, I tried to kiss him because, well, that's what boyfriends and girlfriends were supposed to do. He wasn't too keen and we got into a huge fight. We didn't talk for a few months after. I was really hurt and just couldn't bear to be around him." Staring up at the ceiling, she huffs out a frustrated sigh as she swipes away a few more tears. She lets an amused laugh go and her shoulders sag with relief.

"I don't know how I didn't see it before we dated, but I guess when you're best friends with someone you just get so used to who they are that you don't question anything about them. They're always there, no matter who they are."

"What happened, Lizzy?" Even though I'm pretty sure I know where this is going, I want to hear it from her.

"I was the first person he ever came out to." She cries a little more and slumps down in her seat. "I think he knew for a long time, but our 'dating' forced him to admit it even to himself. He made me promise not to tell anyone and I never did. Until…"

More tears and sobs. More pieces fall together. More ugliness in a world when it's the last thing any of us needs.

"A few of the guys on the football team got suspicious. Something about Cane not wanting to change in the locker room. Apparently when they approached him about it, they didn't like the way Cane answered their questions, so they accused him of being gay. I can only imagine how scared he felt. His deepest secret was suddenly exposed to the meanest and least understanding people in the school."

"Was this when you started calling us?" I hand her another tissue, and squeeze her tiny hand offering her some kind of reassurance that she did the right thing.

"Yeah. He told me what happened and that he was afraid for his own safety. He started talking about running away and I didn't know what to do. When I saw you and Mr. Hopkins at the school last month, I followed you out to the parking lot. I saw you get into this Jeep. Then today, I saw the Jeep drive past my house. I only live down that block." She points over her shoulder indicating the road leading down to the college campus. "After this happened," she runs her finger over her nearly swollen-shut eye, "I was just sitting on my front steps, wondering what the hell to do when I saw your car drive past. I didn't mean to scare your wife. I didn't realize it wasn't you driving. I'm real sorry."

Of all the coincidences, I've never been more thrilled to be stuck with Maddy's shit car in all my life. Without it, Lizzy and I never would have crossed paths.

"So can you tell me about how that happened?" Considering the damage to her face, I should have called the cops the second I saw her.

"Those football guys that I told you about…"

"They didn't touch you?" Anger bubbles deep in my chest and I clench my fists until my knuckles are white with tension.

"No, it was a group of their girlfriends. They said that I needed to keep my fag in line and stop him from hitting on their boys." I hear her cringe on the word "fag" and I can recall the venomous words that fell from my father's mouth the last time I saw him.

"They beat the crap out of me and told me the guys did the same to Cane. I've been trying to call him since after school, but he's not picking up his phone. I'm so scared." Lizzy wraps her arms around her waist, a vain effort to comfort herself through her returning cries.

"It's okay, Lizzy. We'll figure it out." Even though I want to believe the words I've just spoken, I'm not so sure about how to fix this. I'm not sure that it can even be fixed.

"You stay in here and I'm going to make a few calls. Try calling Cane again and call your parents to let them know where you are. And try his parents too. Maybe they've heard from him." She nods and focuses on the tasks I've just given her. Having something to do seems to help her calm down a little more.

I call the cops and let them know where we are and what happened. They're sending the closest dispatch car and it should be here in less than five minutes. Next, I call Dylan who is more than a little relieved at finally having figured out who the caller has been. He's also on his way and should be with us in just a few minutes. I call Momma last and let her know that we might not be there to get Braden in time to put him to bed. Of course, she's never put out to spend more time with him, so she gladly offers to help out and take him overnight.

Sirens blare and lights blaze as a few cop cars pull into the lot. Lizzy and Cane's parents are next to arrive. Concern weighs heavily on all of their faces. In a panicked frenzy, Dylan pulls into the lot last. He offers whatever insight he can into the calls he received and the information that we have from the school, including the principal's number.

By the time Maddy's final ends, we're still in the lot and she's completely shocked by the scene before her. "Is everything alright?" She drops her bag to the ground and stands next to me. We both look on as Lizzy talks to Cane's parents. Everyone's eyes are red and puffy from the cold and the tears.

"It's not okay just yet, but they're working on it." I explain that the police have already filed a missing person report and have also called the parents of the football players and their girlfriends to bring them in for questioning. They're not too confident that the other kids, or their parents for that matter, will be all too cooperative, but they have to start somewhere.

By the time everyone leaves, I'm more than exhausted. "You did a good thing tonight, Reid. Lizzy was really scared and you helped her. I'm proud of you, babe."

Burying my face into her neck, I squeeze her as tight as I can and let her strength seep into my bones. "I just hope they can find him before he does something stupid. It's just not fair."

Maddy cups my jaw and her teary eyes stare sadly into mine. "No, it's not, baby. But you just made it a little bit fairer. Come on, let's get you home. I'll even make you dinner."

I waggle an eyebrow at her and she swats at my chest. "You mean you'll make me cereal, right?"

"Nah, tonight I'll splurge. You get grilled cheese and tomato soup. Nothing but the best for my guy." Her playfulness and sarcasm help to lighten my mood, just a little, and I have to admit that her bright, smiling face plants a seed of hope that maybe things will turn out okay.

CHAPTER SEVEN

Maddy

Watching my two men play trains together on Christmas morning has to be the highlight of my year. Reid was up so late last night putting everything together, so of course, Braden knocked it down in all of two seconds. Reid hooks together two trains and shows Braden how to drive them up and over the hills and mountains. Braden's face lights up and he makes "choo-choo" noises as he shuffles around the waist-high train table. When a train falls off the tracks and crashes into the floor, driving itself under the TV stand, Braden says "uh-oh" and throws his hands in the air.

"I got it buddy." Daddy to the rescue as always.

When he hands the train back to Braden, he sets him back up at the table and looks at me over his shoulder. Of course, he's just caught me staring at him.

His ass was just in my face. Kinda difficult to ignore that.

He slides next to me on the floor and I kiss him on the cheek as I hand him his coffee.

"You look really happy this morning. And Braden loves his train. You did real good, Daddy." He drapes an arm around my shoulders and we share a moment just watching our son drive his trains.

"I am happy." He gives me a tight squeeze.

I know that part of his happiness has also come from the fact that we got a huge break on the Cane case the other night. The girls who beat up Lizzy confessed, under direction of their parents' lawyers, of course. They were kicked off the cheerleading squad since the school has zero tolerance for bullying. Having to do fifty hours of community service barely seems like a sufficient sentence, but at least they aren't going to get away with it entirely.

The football guys, on the other hand, well it looks like they will. I mean without Cane coming forward to say what happened, there isn't much that anyone can do.

"Where'd you go?" Reid looks at me as I'm lost thinking about where Cane is. I don't want to bring it up, being Christmas and all, but I can still see the worry on Reid's face, the lines of tension creasing the corners of his usually bright blue eyes.

"Nowhere. I was just thinking of how happy I am too."

We sit and watch Braden for a few more minutes before the phone rings and Reid gets up to answer it.

"Hey, Dyl. Yeah, Merry Christmas to you too."

Braden chooses this moment to start throwing a mini-tantrum, his cries making it somewhat impossible for Reid to talk on the phone. After I hear him ask Dylan to hang on a minute, he turns to me. "It's about

Cane. I'll be right back in." My stomach twists in knots as I watch him walk down the hall to our room.

In the few minutes that he's in our bedroom, I create all kinds of crazy scenarios about where Cane is and what happened to him. Most of them are just too scary to focus on for more than the briefest of seconds. Even though I try to distract myself with Braden, driving trains and making silly faces, I can't shake the feeling that something horrible happened.

I shoot up from the floor when I hear Reid walking back out to us. "What did he say? What's going on?"

"He's okay." On those two simple words, I see the weight fall from his shoulders, the lines around his eyes smooth, instantly.

I band my arms around his waist burying my face in his chest. "Oh, Reid. That's amazing. Where is he? Did he come back home?"

Reid pulls me over to the couch holding me in place on his lap. "Cane ran away to his aunt and uncle's house. Took the train there in the middle of the night. It turns out that he came out to them over the summer and they said if he ever needed anything, he could go to them, so he did."

I lace our fingers together and run my thumb over his wrist. "Was he hurt?" I ask tentatively, not sure if I really want to know the answer.

"No, thank God," he sighs a deep breath of relief. I know this is what was keeping Reid up at night, wondering if Cane was safe. "The guys never got a hold of him, but he's too scared to come back. Dylan just heard from Lizzy this morning that Cane moved in with his aunt and uncle and he's going to finish out the school year in the new district."

"Reid...that's...really good news." A tear streaks down my cheek, shed in happiness that things turned out the way they did.

"Yeah, it's pretty great actually."

We sit together for a few more minutes, not saying anything, enjoying the sight of our innocent little boy.

"There's still a few more presents under there." Reid tips his chin towards the tree and pulls me down to the floor. Since I'm never one to argue about getting gifts, I go all too willingly.

"This is for you, babe," he smirks as he hands me a not-so-perfectly wrapped box. I give him the stink-eye playfully mocking his sub-par wrapping skills. "Don't look at me like that. He helped," he adds, pointing at Braden who is still blissfully unaware of anything other than his trains.

I can tell by the wrinkles and crumpled corners exactly how Braden "helped."

I shred through the paper and actually gasp as I uncover the book hidden under the wrinkled paper.

"Oh, Reid. It's beautiful." I trace my fingers over the hardcover image of Braden as newborn, swaddled in a pale blue blanket. I remember taking the picture the morning after that first night. Reid laughed at me then, saying that if I woke him up, he was my responsibility. I just shrugged and snapped away. I knew that he wouldn't be this tiny and this peaceful forever and I wanted to capture that moment. And now, my sweet man has captured it forever.

"Do you like it?" he asks cautiously, which is ridiculous.

"I love it, Reid." I can't manage more than that as I start flipping through the pages. Reid has captured the entire journey of us becoming a family right here in these pages. Early sonogram pictures, to my growing belly, the baby shower and then the three of us in the delivery room, just moments after Braden was born.

It's the history of our little family.

"Thank you, baby. It's the best gift ever," I mumble against his lips as I wrap my arms around his neck. I catch a glimmer of something in his eyes as he smirks at me. I ignore him and hand him the last of his gifts from under the tree.

"Here, open this one." I slide a small box to Reid and smirk at him. Like the dork that he is, he actually shakes the box when it's fairly clear that nothing more than an envelope is stuffed inside of it. Braden is crawling around the living room vrooming a new car he opened earlier. Like his daddy, the boy loves his cars.

Reid rips at the shiny, red wrapping paper and laughs aloud at the gift inside of it. "*You* got *me* cooking lessons? This is some kind of joke, right?"

"I didn't get them for you, you ass! I got them for me, but seeing as you're the one who has to deal with my cooking, it really is a gift for you, smart ass." I stick my tongue out at him and laugh when Braden starts mimicking me.

"Get over here." Reid grabs me and hauls me onto his lap. "You know that I would eat cereal and soup for the rest of my life. As long as it means that I get to eat with you, I don't care about the food."

"That's sweet and all, but you deserve better. And now, thanks to Kitchen Divas, you'll get it." I wiggle my ass in his lap. "Then there's always dessert, too." Another wiggle makes his jaw tighten and his fingers dig into my hip.

"You're evil, woman," he chides me mockingly as he starts tickling my side.

"Stop! Reid!" The second the word "stop" is out of my mouth, he's got me pinned beneath him. "What? You want me to stop?" He just tickles me more, clearly not intending to stop.

I can barely speak through my laughter. "Reid! No…not my feet…Reid, I'm serious."

"Ohhhh, look at you, big talker. Now, you're serious, huh? Well, so am I!" He changes tactics once again, straddling my hips and locking my arms at my side. It's pointless to try and buck him off me; besides, he'll just enjoy that too much.

Just when I think he's about to stop, he pulls my shirt up, exposing my belly. "Oh no you don't!" I shoot him a serious look to which he just arches an eyebrow. God, why does he look so freaking sexy when he does that.

With a slowness that belies his intent, he lowers his mouth to my belly button and blows the loudest, wettest raspberry. "Come on, B! Help Daddy get Mommy!" And wouldn't you know it, the little bugger listens and crawls over to where Reid has me trapped.

Braden's pudgy little fingers pinch and tickle at my belly and he tries his hardest to blow some raspberries, but all he manages to do is drool on me.

When I'm red faced and barely able to breathe, Reid lets go of my hands and helps me stand. He lifts Braden up and all three of us stand there as our bubbles of laughter subside.

"I'm gonna get you back. You just wait and see," I threaten.

"I can't wait to see you try, Mrs. Connely." He counters with another sexily arched eyebrow and an innocent peck to the cheek.

"Cocky bastard." I swat him playfully on his chest.

"Listen to the mouth on you!" He switches Braden to his other hip, before asking him, "Can you believe Mommy has such a dirty mouth?"

"Me?" I gasp and poke him in the arm. "You have the filthiest mouth ever. His first word is probably going to be F-U-C-K at the rate you say it around here." I spell out the letters just to prove to him that he's worse than I am and then stick out my tongue for added insult—and to up the maturity level, of course.

"Can I make you breakfast, now that we're done with the presents?"

"I doubt you can, but it'll be fun to watch you try." He turns to Braden and holds up his hand to high-five him at my expense and Braden actually manages to hit him on the hand this time—of course, Reid's been practicing with him. They're teaming up on me already, but I can't deny that I love my boys to death.

Making my way into the kitchen, I decide on scrambled eggs. They're fairly easy to make and fairly difficult to screw up. Toast, on the other hand, is apparently my archenemy. Those Kitchen Divas are going to have their work cut out for them.

Over the clanging of the pan and the cracking of shells, I hear Braden and Reid cleaning up the wrapping paper that's strewn about the floor. I catch of glimpse of Reid handing Braden a wad of paper and showing him how to slam-dunk it. When Braden actually makes it into the bag, Reid claps wildly and tosses Braden in the air telling him what a good job he did. Watching Reid with Braden, witnessing the man I love and the child I gave birth to become best friends brings tears to my eyes. It's the most perfect thing to see on Christmas morning.

Of course that bubble of perfection is broken, when Reid hands me the tied up bag of wrapping paper claiming that he needs to go change my son's stinky ass—funny how when he smells, he becomes *my* son. I slide my slippers on and wrap myself in my grey, wool pea coat to take the trash out to the dumpster.

I nearly trip over my own two feet as I step out the front door. Mouth agape, bag dropped to the floor, I'm completely speechless as I stare at what I assume is my new car. It has a giant red bow on top of it and everything. The sun's rays sparkle and dance across the shiny, black exterior of the Nissan Murano. Still frozen by both disbelief and the cold, I jump a little when I feel Reid's jacket-covered arm snake around my waist from behind.

"Merry Christmas, baby." I simply stare at him in shock as he dangles the keys in front of me.

He hits a button on the key-fob and the engine purrs. "Reid, you didn't have to..."

"I know I didn't *have* to, but I *wanted to*. So I did. Well actually, we did, right, buddy?" I'm just now noticing that Braden is outside with him, all bundled up of course. The freaking garbage was just a diversion. Smooth. I'll have to give him credit for that one.

"Come on. I want you to see the inside." He loops his arm through mine and pulls me over to the truck. It's gorgeous and I love it instantly. Standing outside of the driver's side door, he hands me the key-fob explaining how the keyless entry and ignition work. He can be such a guy—getting lost in all things cars and sports sometimes—but honestly, all I need to know is that the green circle starts the thing. The rest might as well be in Japanese.

We sit in the front seats for a few minutes, me staring at the clean interior and shiny features while Reid explains what all of the buttons do. There are so many buttons, but I'm sure I'll at least remember the important ones. Just as he's wrapping up his little tutorial, I realize I didn't see my old car in the lot.

"What did you do with the Civic? I can't imagine that you were able to get anything for it?" Knowing Reid, *he* probably had to pay someone to take it off our hands.

"Yeah, that wasn't happening. The dealership wasn't even willing to take it as a trade-in." I figured as much. But as freaking ancient as that car was, I still had some good memories with it. It was really the only thing I ever had from Aunt Maggie, though the fact that my fondest memory of her is of the car she left me is pretty sad.

"So what did you do? Drive it off a cliff like you've been promising to do?"

"Momma told me about a children's cancer center she's worked with before that takes old cars as donations. I guess they fix them up and sell them or something to make money, but I figured since we really weren't going to be able to get more than ten or fifteen bucks for it, I might as well just give it to someone who could actually get something out of it." He shrugs his shoulders deflecting the praise he knows is coming.

There have been a handful of moments in my life, that have really defined who I am—that have really altered the way I view the world. This is one of them. Time and time again, Reid reminds me that there is genuine kindness and love in world that is so often filled with ugliness and hatred.

Leaning over the center console, I cup his jaw reveling in the feel of his rough stubble scratching at my fingertips. "You're a good man, Reid." I softly press my lips against his as Braden wiggles in his lap clearly getting fidgety and probably a little hungry. "I love you and thank you for this. It's too much, but I love it."

"Anything for you, Maddy. Anything in the world." We share one more kiss before stepping out of the car.

Reid takes care of the trash while I take Braden inside to get him his breakfast. We have a few hours to spend together at home before we head over to Momma's for Christmas dinner. Melanie and Bryan will be there. Since he lives there now, so will Evan too. Dylan will be joining us as well and considering all of the stuff that happened the other day with Lizzy and Cane, I hope he'll be in better spirits.

Knowing better than to ask us to bring anything really important, I was assigned the task of making the cheese and cracker platter. Yep, it's pretty clear to see that Momma has very little faith in my cooking abilities. Though, I can't say I blame her too much. Sending someone to the hospital with food poisoning is not the best way to celebrate Christmas.

*****

Sometime close to midnight, we leave Momma's. The day was filled with good food, hearty laughter and happy memories. Braden is fast sleep within five minutes of being strapped into his car seat and about two minutes after that, I feel my eyes begin to droop with heavy sleep.

The icy cold blast from the door opening makes my teeth chatter. I grumble in protest at the gentle nudge I feel on my shoulder. "We're home, Maddy. You take Braden, and I'll get the rest of the stuff." Since we changed him into his feetie pajamas before we left, all I really need to do is change his diaper quickly and tuck him in. He's had such a busy and exciting day that I doubt he'll put up much of a fuss.

When I successfully change him without a peep, I have to stifle a laugh remembering those early diaper changes. I didn't believe her then, but she was right— Momma ~~usually~~ always is. I did get more comfortable with him; we did develop our own routine. Things did get easier.

Braden nuzzles into the crook of my neck as I sing him a sweet lullaby before tucking him under his blankies. Just as I close the door to his nursery, I hear Reid step back outside for one last trip to the car. That leaves me just enough time to get my surprise present for him ready.

Seeing as we kind of did this whole marriage and a kid thing backwards, and at a ridiculously early age, we never really had much of a 'honeymoon' phase.

This last gift will help to make up for that. At least, I hope it will.

After grabbing my things, I slip into the bathroom as I hear the front door close one last time. Reid lightly taps on the door. "I'll be right out, hun."

After I hear his footsteps drift away from the door, I open up the Victoria's Secret bag and step out of my clothes. The satiny smooth fabric of the black silk and lace chemise slides over my skin, hugging the curve of my hips. Both side panels of the lingerie are sheer, black lace—almost completely see through. The tops of my breast are mostly exposed. I'm pretty sure if I take a really deep breath, they'll fall out completely. I step into black sheer stockings and clip the lacey tops to the garter belt. Smoothing the fabric out one last time, I check myself in the mirror. I have to say, that even though my body has changed so much in the last year and a half, I look hot and I feel sexy.

A quick fluff of my hair, a swipe of some sheer lip gloss, a spray of perfume and I'm ready to go. One last touch—four inch, red, peep-toe heels. Yeah, I'm good to go now.

I'm careful to tiptoe across the hallway, conscious not to make any noise with the clicking of my heels on the old, beat-up hardwood floors. Waking up Braden is the last thing I want to do.

Quietly, I push open the door. Reid doesn't hear me because he doesn't turn around immediately. He's standing in front of the dresser unbuttoning the cuffs from his dress shirt. Watching him toy with his wedding band before slipping it off his finger is sensual and arousing as I imagine his fingers sliding into me. Leaning up against the doorframe, I clear my throat to get his attention.

When he turns to face me, I can actually see his ice-blue eyes blaze with lust. The muscles in his neck tense as he clenches his jaw. The cords of his shoulders bunch and pull as he removes his undershirt and tosses it on the bed. Silently, with predatory stealth, he struts over to me. Without saying a word, he runs his nose from my shoulder up the column of my neck, stopping only to pull my earlobe in between his teeth.

Sliding his hands over the cool fabric of the nightie, he nearly groans in pleasure. "You like?" I roll my head to the side and he nibbles on the sensitive spot where my neck meets my shoulder. Toying with the thin spaghetti strap, he lets it fall off my shoulder. He takes a step back and inspects my outfit—though I'm pretty sure he doesn't actually need to look at it again to know that he loves it.

"Like?" His throat shifts as he swallows, hard. "I've never seen you in anything like this." His hands roam over my back and he cups my ass.

"You didn't answer me. Do you like it?" A seductive look takes over my face and my lips curl into a devilish smile. I know he more than *likes* it, but I just want to hear him say it.

Slowly, he moves his hands from my ass and runs his fingertips up the lacy sides, causing a shiver of pleasure to follow in their wake. My nipples pucker instantly straining against the satin.

Reid brushes his knuckles over my diamond hard tips, gently grazing over them oh-so-lightly. "No, Maddy. I don't *like* it." He hefts the full weight of my tits and then pinches the stiff peaks of my nipples. "I fucking *love* it."

Without warning, he begins fucking my mouth with his tongue. The kiss is hot and wildly passionate. Reid is in pure alpha mode and I love it. He nips and bites at my lips, sucks on my tongue and tastes every single inch of my mouth. Snaking my arms around his neck, I tug the hair that curls at the nape.

In an instant, he's got his hands around my waist, effortlessly lifting me up onto the edge of the dresser. His biceps bulge and my mouth goes dry at the sight of his hard chest.

With my ass on the edge of the dresser, Reid stands in between my legs. Running his fingers over my arms once more causes another round of shivers to run across my flesh. He lowers his head to my breasts and licks a heated path across the satiny edge of the fabric. Through the thin fabric, he pulls a taut nipple into his hot mouth. My head rolls back and a contented sigh passes through my lips. When he blows a cool breath on my breast, I roll my hips forward searching for some kind of relief from the surge of pressure he just set loose.

After he does the same to the other nipple, he pulls both straps down my shoulders and off my arms completely, fully exposing my breasts. Pinching, rolling, pulling, kneading, sucking – he assaults my breasts and it's a delicious combination of pleasure and pain.

His rough hands skim up my thighs pushing the fabric up around my waist. He stands, frozen to the spot, when he catches sight of what he's just unveiled. Tracing the line of the garter belt, under which there are no panties, I can see him trying to restrain himself.

"I have no clue what the fuck this is," he pulls at the edge of the garment, "but it's the hottest fucking thing I have *ever* seen. If it was up to me, you would wear this and only this every single day."

I arch my hips as much as I can, given the small space on which I'm perched, to give him a better view. He growls when he sees my lips, swollen and wet, beckoning for him to touch. "Damn, you're gorgeous, Maddy."

With a whisper soft touch, he glides the pad of his thumb over the seam of my lips, avoiding my clit. I push forward, trying to get his hand to go where I want it. It's futile though.Reid is in charge. He owns my body and I let him. It's a perfect symphony of give and take, touch and tease.

After a few more languorous strokes of my pussy, he pushes two fingers inside and swirls them around, instantly bringing me to the brink of pleasure, the edge of reason. With his other hand, he pushes my thighs apart. "Open for me. Fuck my hand," he commands with a gruff rasp in his voice. Supporting some of my weight on my hands, I lift my ass from the surface and move my hips in rhythm with his hand. "So good, Reid," I moan and grumble, the pull and drag of his fingers hitting my clit on every thrust.

All too abruptly, he removes his hand from deep inside of me. "That was fucking hot," he says, before licking his fingers clean. "And you're fucking delicious." Lifting me once more, he carries me over to the bed. I feel the hardness of his cock push into me as I wrap my legs around his waist. When he drops me on the mattress, I feel bereft of his heat, longing for more.

I watch in silence as he unsnaps his pants and pushes them, along with his boxers, down over his narrow hips and muscular thighs. Toeing off his shoes and socks, he stands before me—beautifully naked and *very* ready for action. I cross my legs and reach to pull my shoe off. His voice cuts through the room. "Leave them on."

Sliding the sexy red pump back in place, Reid stares at me, penetratingly, almost like a wild beast.

"Roll over." His roughened command takes me by surprise and causes a surge of wetness. I comply, of course, even though my pulse is racing. The mattress dips as he kneels in between my legs, nudging them wider. His finger trails down the length of my spine, stopping only when it meets the edge of the fabric that stops just beneath the dimples of my lower back. Flipping the short skirt up over my ass, he bunches the fabric around my waist.

Rough palms scorch the sensitized skin of my inner thighs as he pushes me up onto my knees. Hot lips kiss each cheek before playful teeth gently sink into my flesh.

Banding one arm around my hips, he plays with my pussy, flicks at my clit from behind. I feel his cock pressing into the softness of my ass. "Please, baby, I need you," I call out desperately

All the control and dominance he had vanishes when he hears my needy words. Lacing his fingers together with mine, he stretches our arms above my head. His hard chest presses into my back, the light dusting of hair tickling my hot skin.

He rolls us so that we're both on our sides, my back to his front. Holding my knee in the crook of his elbow, he angles his hips forward and sinks into me from behind. With his other hand wrapped around my chest, he teases my nipples with his strong fingers. When his hand moves around my neck, seductively holding me in place, my pussy flutters out of pure ecstasy.

"Maddy...oh God," he grumbles into my neck. "I can feel you...God, I can feel you clamp down on me. Come, baby." As if he doesn't trust me to obey his command, he removes his hand from my neck and trails it down in between my legs.

A few brushes against my clit and I fall, coming wildly. My hips thrust without any rhythm whatsoever. Fire spreads through my belly as Reid pulls me hard against his chest.

"Fuck, Maddy. I can't hold off any longer."

With a few more erratic thrusts, Reid growls out as his orgasm pours into me.

He sweeps my hair to the side and kisses my neck. Resting my cheek against his bent arm, I nuzzle into him inhaling his purely masculine scent.

After a few long moments, our breathing calms. I kick my shoes off, and even though I'm completely incapable of moving, I sit up so I can get rid of what little clothing I have on. Reid tosses me one of his T-shirts and gathers my black satin and lace garments from the floor.

"These are definitely going to have to make another appearance, real soon," he smirks as he tosses them into the laundry basket.

When we're curled around one another in bed, a sense of calm peacefulness fills the room. Our son is sleeping quietly in the next room and we just had wild, crazy, monkey sex without waking him up. I guess we're getting good at this parenting stuff, after all.

I laugh out loud at that thought.

"What's so funny over there?" Reid pops a kiss to the top of my head and squeezes my shoulder.

"I was just thinking how crazy insane it is that we just did *that* and didn't wake him up."

"Shh. Don't jinx it." We share a laugh and I begin tracing random patterns in his chest hair, following the inky, black lines of his tatted pecs.

"Can I ask you something?"

He looks down at me wary of my randomness. "Of course, sweets. Anything."

"Do you ever think of having another one, a baby, I mean."

His hand stills on my shoulder and I feel him hold his breath, his chest tense under my hand.

"Relax, Reid. I didn't mean today or tomorrow. I just meant sometime in the future."

His hand resumes tickling my skin as he presses his lips to my forehead. "You're not popping one out tomorrow, right?" he jokes, but I hear the seriousness there. I shake my head and he chuckles. "Well, in that case, yes." I poke him in the ribs at his sarcastic tone.

Cupping my jaw and staring intently into my eyes, he brushes his lips against mine. "Yes, Maddy. I want to have more babies with you. I want to have a big family. I want us to be the family that neither of us ever had."

My heart swells for my man and his sweetness. "You mean you don't think it's crazy we're both barely in our twenties and we're talking about having *another* baby?"

A dopey smile lifts at the corners of his mouth. "Yeah, sure it's crazy. I can't imagine that things will get less crazy, but I know way down to my bones, that there is no one I'd rather go crazy with."

"You're amazing, you know that?" I smile up at him, his deep blue eyes alight with humor.

"Yep, I sure am. But it's only because I have you."

"Now, you're just laying it on thick, Connely." I poke him in the ribs again.

"Is it working?" he quips.

Even though the room is dark, I roll my eyes and say nothing.

"I thought so." I feel his smile against my temple as he presses his lips there one more time.

Spring
May 2015

~

EPILOGUE

Maddy

"I feel like a dork." I look at Melanie who is sitting behind me on my bed. Adjusting my graduation cap and tassel one last time, I zipper up my gown and hold my arms out to the side.

"Yep, you look like one too. A dork with a diploma though." Mel's freckled face splits with a proud smile.

"It's only junior college. Not a big deal." Shrugging, I sit next to her and slide my feet into black, strappy sandals.

"It is so a big deal. Besides, trying telling Mom that. She's practically rolled out the red carpet for you." Mel reaches into her bag next to her on the bed. "Here. I got you a little something."

"Melanie, you didn't have to." She shoots me the *best friend* slash *shut your mouth* look and I tear into the paper.

"Oh, Mel. It's gorgeous." I trace my fingers over the silver letters that spell out "sisters" across the cover of an absolutely stunning scrapbook. "Did you make this?"

"Yes, I did. I wanted you to have something special today." She squeezes me tightly and scoots right next to me so we can look through the pictures together.

I'm rendered speechless at her thoughtfulness. Carefully selecting pictures of both of us, from when we were babies all the through just last weekend at a backyard barbeque, she has created a timeline of both of our lives. We'll never be sisters by blood, but looking through this album—seeing the two of us all dressed up for prom, goofing off at sleepovers, and dancing at my wedding—we'll never be anything but sisters by choice.

We both swipe at the tears of happiness flowing down our cheeks. "Come on. We better get going. Everyone is out there waiting for us." We share in one last sisterly embrace before walking out to the living room where Momma, Evan, Bryan, Braden and Reid are waiting for us. Katie and Joe even made the trip out to celebrate.

A chorus of cheers and claps great me. Braden races up to me, calling out "Mommy! Mommy!"

"Hey sweet boy!" I lift him up to my hip and Reid stands next to me. Making eye contact with everyone else, I smile and fight back a few tears. "Thank you for being here guys. I don't know what to say."

"There's nothing to say. We're here because we love you and we're extremely proud of you." Momma hugs me and hands me a tissue. Evan stands beside us, smiling proudly. "We both are, Maddy. A college degree is a huge accomplishment. Lucy and I are very proud of everything you've done."

It's silly really, but hearing Evan say those things, feeling Momma's arms wrapping around my shoulders, makes me feel like I've been given back the parents I lost so long ago.

Scanning the room, I realize that one very important person is missing. "Hey, where's Dylan? I thought he was meeting us here?"

"He was supposed to, but Lizzy showed up at the center today with a letter from Cane." Reid's words silence the room.

"What?" I gasp. "When? Why didn't you tell me? What happened? Is everything okay?" My questions come out rapid-fire style, frantic and obviously concerned.

"Yes, everything is fine." Good, he decided to answer the most important question first. He sees my shoulders slump and rubs my back to ease the tension. Even though he's been in relative safety living with his aunt and uncle, we've all been concerned that he's really okay.

"So then what happened?" Bryan chimes in. Having always taken an interest in Reid's work with bullied kids, he was really affected by Cane and Lizzy's situation. When Cane ran away and no one heard from him in that first week, Bryan actually helped out down at The Bridge stuffing envelopes and making calls.

"Well, it was a good update actually. He sent Lizzy his graduation picture. Dylan said Cane looks healthy, really happy too." A collective sigh of relief fills the room. "He's adjusted pretty well there, apparently. Lizzy just needed someone to talk to, so he said he would meet us there later."

"That's really great news, Reid." Bryan claps him on the shoulder.

"Yeah, I know we were all expecting the worst. Hopefully, it continues to work out for him. He's too young to be afraid to live his life." Reid takes Braden from my arms and kisses him sweetly. "Dylan and Lizzy have been meeting a lot over the last few months, so he wanted to be there to support her today. He said she was really upset, missing him and all." Reid shrugs like what he and Dylan do on a regular basis with these kids is not that big of a deal. But it is. I try to convince him that what they do is nothing short of amazing, but I know there's a part of him that still won't give himself the credit he deserves.

Joe sees it too. I notice him smiling through Reid's update on Lizzy and Cane. "Good job, son." Not afraid to show his emotions, Joe hugs Reid with the fatherly pride that he's deserved all his life.

Katie takes Braden from Reid and whispers something in his ear before turning to the rest of us. "I'm going to go put this little guy in the car. We better hit the road if we want to get to the college on time." She taps the face of her watch and everyone else falls in line.

I grab my bag as Reid grabs his keys from the dish on our entryway table. "What did Katie just say to you?" I ask, straightening my cap one last time.

He gulps before smiling, his eyes crinkling in the corners. "She said that Mom would be proud of me."

"Oh, baby. You know she would be. So would Shane." Standing next to him, we gaze at the framed faces of those we have loved and lost. I wrap my arm around his waist as he kisses my hair.

Cars honk out in front of the apartment, our cue to get our butts in gear, but I call him back into the living room as his hand hovers above the doorknob.

"Reid. Wait. I have something for you today." Nervousness makes my voice tremble.

"For me? But you're the one graduating." He grins goofily as he tucks his sunglasses into the slightly opened collar of his dress shirt.

I hand him his present, a small rectangular box, like one in which you would put a piece of jewelry.

After ripping open the paper, he cracks open the box and stares at me, dumbfounded. "Re-gifting already?" He arches an eyebrow as he pulls the necklace that he gave me on our first Christmas together out of the box.

"Not really. Look closer." I take the necklace out of his hands and repeat the words he said to me once before.

"This one is for you," I say as I hold the charm with "R" engraved on it. "And this one is for me. This next one is for Braden," I let the fourth charm slip out

of my palm where it was concealed. "And *this* one—"
His lips stop my words.

Smiling against my lips, he wraps his arms
around my waist and spins me in the air. "Really?" His
voice is shaking with emotion.

"Yes, really," I smile lamely, hopeful that he's
not upset.

"But we only…"

"I know. We only just decided, but I guess
we're just that lucky." We've talked about it in the last
month or so and decided that despite the challenges it
might pose to our careers and my schooling, it was
more important to give Braden a sibling close to him in
age.

"Damn straight we're lucky!" He kisses me
again and I can tell he's anything but upset.

"Maybe it'll be a girl." I'm not-so-secretly
hoping for that to be true, but when I see genuine fear
dance across Reid's beautiful face, I have to laugh at
him.

More honks interrupt our little bubble. "Okay,
so that's a 'maybe' on the whole girl thing," I joke
playfully poking him in the side.

"I'd be the luckiest man on Earth to have a
daughter. Hell, I'm already the luckiest man alive to
share my life with you." Lacing our fingers together, he
brings our joined hands up to his lips and kisses my
knuckles.

"I'm pretty damn lucky too, babe." We share one last hug before deciding to hold off on telling everyone else for now.

Today, we'll celebrate one chapter of our lives coming to a close, and tonight, well, I guess tonight, we'll celebrate another chapter of our lives beginning.

THE END

ACKNOWLEDGEMENTS

There are so many people who have been an integral part of helping me get this series off and running. My family and friends, the indie author community, countless blogs and promoters, but there would be no point to writing these stories if I didn't have the most amazing readers out there. With that in mind, I'm dedicating this book to you – my fans. You have been so amazingly supportive reaching out to me with messages and leaving reviews. I am in awe of your love for Maddy and Reid and all of my other characters. You bring these characters to life and I am more thankful than I can express for wanting more of them.

SOCIAL MEDIA LINKS

Facebook - http://www.facebook.com/MelissaCollins.Author

Twitter - @mcollinsauthor

Pinterest – www.pinterest.com/mcollinsauthor

Be sure to sign up for my newsletter so you don't miss a single Love Series update

www.melissacollinsauthor.com

Turn the page for 7 bonus scenes from *Let Love In* and *Let Love Stay*

BONUS SCENE #1

Alternate POV from Let Love In

When Reid meets Maddy for the first time

"Thirteen, fourteen, fifteen."

I heft the one-hundred-and-seventy-five-pound weight above my head for one last bench press. My chest burns and I'm going to be fucking sore tomorrow, but I don't mind the after effects. Jake, my spotter and gym buddy, helps me place the bar in its holder and I slide from under it and off the bench.

"Thanks, man," I say to him as I wipe the sweat from my face with a small towel. "I think I'm done for the night." My words are winded from the exertion.

"Yeah, I'm good too." Jake rubs his biceps, which have to be sore after two hours of arm and upper body workouts.

As we clean up our workout area and head over to the locker room, Jake asks, "So what are your plans tonight? Got anything going on?" He swipes his towel over his short-cropped brown hair.

Twisting the dial on the combination lock on my locker, I say, "There's a party at the house, again. So I'll probably find *something* to do." I think the smirk on my face conveys exactly what I mean.

"And by *something* you mean *someone*, right?" Jake laughs and punches me in the arm.

Jake and I have been friends since freshman year and we go to the gym pretty regularly. He usually makes an appearance at my parties and he also finds *something*, and yes by that, I mean *someone,* to occupy his time, but his most recent hook-up turned into a pretty steady thing.

"Oh, cut the shit. You were all about the newest *someone* until Jocelyn came along. Now you're all wifed-up. So if anything, *I* should be giving *you* shit!" I push him knocking him slightly off balance and he almost falls off the bench that runs between the two rows of lockers.

Recovering his balance and pulling his hoodie out from his locker, he turns to me. "Whatever, man. At least I know I'll be getting some tonight and I don't have to waste my energy playing some chick just so I can get laid!" he scoffs as he slides his gym bag over his shoulder.

I get the last of my things out of my locker and pull my bag across my chest. Jake's words echo in my thoughts. I'll never admit it to him aloud, but he's partially right. Three years of playing the game—being all douchey and aloof, being in permanent "I don't care" mode—is exhausting. I'm still shocked that so many girls are attracted to it.

Can someone say Daddy issues?

As Jake and I walk across the quad to the parking lot, he continues his ribbing. "Seriously, dude. You can fuck around with me all you want about being with Jocelyn, but at least I know who I'm waking up with."

I roll my eyes and slap him on his back. "That is where you're wrong, my friend. I know exactly who I'll be waking up with." He eyes me suspiciously like I've just confessed a huge secret. "Chill the fuck out. I just meant that I'll be waking up alone. You know I never let the 'One Nighters' stay over." How could he forget my number one rule!

He shakes his head in disgust. "Whatever. Maybe I'll catch you later."

"Sure thing." We do the whole fist-bump-and-slap-on-the-back dude handshake thing and he stalks off to his car.

Never in a million years did I ever envision Jake being the one to give me relationship advice, or whatever the hell that just was. Jake was an even bigger player than me in his prime. Then Jocelyn came into his life and it was like a complete turnaround. In all of my disillusioned wisdom, the only reason I can muster up is that she must be fucking amazing in bed.

As I approach my car, I see someone leaning up against it. It's Jessa. Thoughts of Jake and his pussy-whipped mentality vanish immediately. The only thing I can think of in this moment is Jessa bent over the side of my bed as I drill into her from behind. That's how we spent last weekend, anyway.

Even though I can't stand her, I can't deny that she looks fucking smoking hot. She's a pain in the ass, clingy as fuck and all that, but she's a good lay. As I get closer to her, I take in her long, skinny legs, which are barely covered in the too-short-to-be-worn-in-public mini skirt. The skirt, along with her extremely miniscule top, makes her look more like a prostitute than a college student. She must be on the prowl.

"Hey sexy," she purrs as I approach her. Sometimes I just wish she would cut the shit and just get to the point.

I nod my head curtly in her direction. "Hey yourself. What are you doing here?" She's clingy and I hate it, but I tone down my words. I could use a good lay.

She moves away from the car and straightens her skirt. Even straightened, it still doesn't cover much.

Probably won't even have to take it off. Slide that right up over her ass, move the thong to the side, fuck her and send her on her way. Won't even have to wait for her to get dressed again.

My dick throbs at the thought.

"I was hoping we could get together later." She's trying to be coy. Like her fucking outfit and body language aren't already screaming "I want to fuck!".

"Sure. Whatever. Stop by the house later. There's a party." She leans into me seductively, like my words were just some kind of magical foreplay or something like that. See what I mean, be a dick and they come flocking.

She runs her hands over my chest and reaches up on her toes. Pressing her lips against my neck, she whispers, "You got it, babe. I'll see you for more of this," she traces her tongue along my neck and nibbles on my earlobe indicating what she means by *this*, "later."

She struts off in front of me purposefully swaying her ass and hips. I have to laugh at her over-the-top behavior. If she only knew that I don't really care how the hell she acts, as long as she spreads her legs, which she never seems to have a problem doing, then I'm fine.

It's a shame none of these girls realize that sex is all I'm after with them. No one is getting close *ever*. That's how it's been for the last four years, and as long as I have any control over it, that's how it will remain for the foreseeable future.

When I pull up to the house ten minutes later, the party is already in full swing. Either these things are starting earlier or I'm staying at the gym later. I park my car far enough from the chaos that is our driveway. I don't want anyone to fuck up my car.

Walking through the living room and into the kitchen, I don't see Jack anywhere. He must be out back. I think I remember him saying something about Cammie and her new roommates coming over tonight. I'm going to have to avoid them at all costs. Clingy freshmen who make it their life's mission to get to know everything about everyone they meet is the most fucking annoying thing ever. I like not knowing anything about anyone. I'm even happier to know that no one knows anything about me.

As I walk into the kitchen, I notice a few guys from Jack's PT program doing shots along the counter and I nod a "hey" in their direction. They don't hold my attention for long, though. As my gaze falls to the ass that's bopping up and down from behind the refrigerator door, the rest of the room fades away.

That's one seriously fine ass. Now, I've got my back-up if things fall through with Jessa tonight.

I slide in behind her and notice that her tight ass is attached to tiny waist. Her legs are to die for and I can't help but think about them wrapped around my hips or up around my ears—either will work for me.

When she turns around and crashes into my chest, the scent of her hair invades my nose and scatters my brain. Light and citrusy, she literally smells like a breath of fresh air. I just shake it off. I mean what guy doesn't love the smell of a gorgeous woman.

Hmmm, I wonder what the rest of her smells like.

"Hand me one?" My voice catches a little in my throat as I try to take in her face. She's fucking beautiful. Bright green eyes, a perfect little nose, but what's most disarming is the look of shock as I catch her off-guard. If I'm not mistaken, she might have actually blushed when I spoke. Do girls actually blush?

Most of the girls I've known aren't embarrassed by much of anything—blushing and embarrassment aren't part of their behavior.

"Here you go." Her voice is soft and sweet. It quivers with uncertainty and it does some serious damage to my game. Not knowing exactly how to react to this sweet creature in front of me, I chug down my bottle of water to avoid having to say anything. I swipe my arm across my mouth to wipe away the water that's dripping down my chin.

It's water. Not drool.

Her eyes rake ravenously over my body. She likes what she sees, most of them do.

"Thanks…" My sentence ends abruptly. I don't know her name. Waiting for her to fill in the blank, I eye her up and down. She's beautiful, perfect really. I quirk my eyebrow up at her prompting her to tell me her name.

She finally catches onto my unasked question. "Maddy. Sorry, my name is Maddy." I can't suppress the lopsided grin which curls up the corner of my lips. Her voice is so shaky and unsure. It's been so long since a girl has been caught off-guard with me, since someone has been real around me, that I almost don't know what to do with it.

She continues talking to me and I have a hard time focusing on her words. All I see are her soft, full lips moving quickly, trying to explain her presence. "My suite mate, Cammie, is dating one of the guys who live here," she says.

Hmmm. So maybe hanging around with Jack and Cammie tonight might actually pay off.

I realize I still haven't said anything to her earlier statement. I'm still lost in the thought of what her lips taste like, what her creamy skin would look like if I could make her blush all over.

"I'm not that much of a drinker so I hope you don't mind if I steal one of these from you?" She's so freaking adorable. Wait. Did I just think that a girl was adorable? What the fuck?

Returning to my standard dickishness, I say, "Help yourself. It's just water. I'm going to go grab a shower. Maybe I'll see you later, Maddy." Effectively putting an end to the conversation, I walk away from her and head upstairs to my room. She might be downstairs, but thoughts of her sweet mouth will definitely be accompanying me as I shower.

When I come back downstairs a while later— the shower took a little longer than planned—I see her moving and swaying on the dance floor. Our eyes meet and I'm mesmerized by her body flowing in rhythm to the music. The girl can move. In that moment, I need to feel her body up against mine. I need to know if the real thing lives up to the fantasy I just created in the shower.

Slinking up behind her, I glide my hands over her waist and pull her close to me. Leaning into her hair, I inhale deeply. I can't deny it. I want her.

Leaning in so my lips are no more than a centimeter away from her ear, I say, "I think you owe me a dance."

She turns around sharply, caught off guard by my flirting. "Owe you? For what?" There's so much innocence in her voice that I'm thrown a bit. "For the water of course," I say sweetly.

I register the shock and apology that spreads across her beautiful face, "Oh. I'm sorry. I didn't realize…" I have to laugh. Does she really think I'm pissed about a bottle of water? My God, how fucking cute is that? Okay, something is definitely wrong with me tonight. I've just thought of the words "cute" and "adorable" to describe a girl. I need to walk away now before I'm completely and totally knocked off my game.

I want to walk away, but I can't. I'm drawn to her and this playful banter is kind of fun. I laugh at both her embarrassment and my extremely abnormal behavior.

She looks wounded as I laugh. Before I can even get the words together to explain myself, she places her hands on my chest and leans up on her toes. Close to my ear, so close in fact that chills course through my body, she pitches her voice low and says, "I could pay you back with more than a dance, Reid."

Holy fuck! She's sweet and sexy. This can't be for real.

Quickly regaining my composure, I cock my head to the side. "So you did a little digging, huh?" I need to stay on top here. I've never been out of control like this, but Maddy is fucking killing me here. I've only known her five minutes and already I never know what to expect from her.

"My name—you just had to find out who I am, did you?" I'm messing with her, but I have to admit that part of me is very turned on that she had to figure out who I am.

"Of course I dug. I needed to know who was responsible for getting me all hot and sweaty before." As soon as the words are out of her mouth, she regrets saying them. Heat blooms across her neck and chest; her cheeks turn pink.

Going in for the kill, I put my lips right up against the outer shell of her ear. "So I got you all hot and bothered? Hmmm. Let's see if I can do it again." I pull her onto the makeshift dance floor in the living room and thank fucking God that it's a slow song. Now, I have the perfect excuse to keep her tight ass pressed up against my groin.

When she raises her arms above her head and starts shimmying against my body, I nearly lose it. Needing to feel her skin under my fingertips, I trace lightly over her arms. Her skin flames and my desire for her is out of control. I feel her skin raise as goose bumps cover her arms. When her hands start roaming all over my back and chest, I want nothing more than to take her up to my room.

We move, perfectly in sync with one another. Her soft body pressed up against mine is pure heaven. I spin her around and our eyes meet again.

Fuck. Her eyes are wide but crinkling in the corners. She doesn't have to try all that hard to figure out what I'm thinking. Thousands of unspoken words are exchanged in that one simple stare. I feel vulnerable and exposed. She knows I want her. But what's even scarier is that I do—I want her so badly and not just for one night.

Remembering my vow to myself from so many years ago, I remind myself to keep my walls intact. I have to get away, now, before she figures me out, before I do something I regret.

"Thanks for the dance," I say sharply as I help her stand up straight from the last spin. She tenses at the cold, hard change in my demeanor.

Whatever. I can't risk being hurt again.

As I strut away from her, I see Jessa across the room. Desperate to forget Maddy, I spend the rest of the night making out with Jessa on the couch, certain for Maddy to witness the whole sickening scene.

I want her to see me with Jessa. I want her to be disgusted with me. The more I can piss her off, the more I can guarantee that she'll leave me, and my dark secrets alone.

BONUS SCENE #2

Alternate POV from Let Love In

Maddy wakes up from being drugged in Reid's POV

The movement at my side wakes me up. Reaching my hand the other side of the bed, I feel someone next to me. What the freak? No one ever stays the night. Who the hell? Then, as the fuzziness clears from my head, I remember everything.

Maddy being drugged.

Me saving her.

Tucking her into bed and then sleeping peacefully for the first time in as long as I can remember.

There were no nightmares last night.

I roll over on my side to a wide-eyed and obviously afraid Maddy. Cupping her cheek in my hand, I need to try to calm her down. She looks like a frightened deer caught in the headlights.

"Good morning, beautiful." I don't mean for my words to sound as sugary sweet as they just did, but she really is beautiful, all sleep mussed and drowsy—she looks perfect, really.

Shock is still washing over her as she comes to. "Um, did we…you know." She's flailing her arms all over the place trying to communicate what her words aren't. Finally, she spits out what she's been trying to get at. "Did we…umm…do it?"

Holy fucking shit! She can't even say the word. She's so damn adorable that I can't help but laugh at her. I pull myself up against the headboard and she joins me. She thinks I don't notice, but I see her peaking under the covers to check out her state of undress. I'm pretty damn proud of myself that I didn't touch her last night. God, I wanted to, but even I'm not that much of an asshole.

When she's situated next to me, I stare into her eyes. "No, Maddy. We most definitely did not 'do it.' Believe me *when* we 'do it', you'll remember." I arch an eyebrow at her and fold my arms behind my head.

"Did you just say *when* we sleep together?" Her shock just adds to my desire for her. Does she think that I don't want her? Fuck. I thought I made that pretty clear last night.

"Yes, I did." I'm not going to hide that I want her any more. Seeing her with that dick last night, gutted me. I won't do that again.

"So Maddy, what do you remember from last night?" I hate thinking about what could have happened to her if I wasn't there. I never would have pegged myself as the protective type, but her vulnerability and sweetness have done all sorts of messed-up shit to my head. To be honest, I can't say I hate how I've changed since I met her.

She looks so freaking hot chewing on her lip and twirling her hair as she tries to place what happened. "Um, well I remember being at the pool hall with everyone. And then I remember Mike and I hanging out at the bar for a little bit. After that, things get a little fuzzy."

She's got bits and pieces of the story straight, but the big part, the part about her almost being kidnapped and raped—because I'm certain that's what that guy would have done to her—that part is eluding her memories.

I see her panic rise as some of the big picture comes into focus. She's almost shaking with nervousness. The need to calm her is like needing to take my next breath.

"Don't worry, Maddy. Nothing happened. I was walking back into Shooters when Mike was trying to leave with you. You guys walked past me and I saw that something was off. Your eyes weren't clear. They were all glassy and you just didn't seem with it. I had been watching you all night, so I knew you weren't drunk. That's when I realized he must have slipped you something. I knocked him on his ass and then brought you here. I know you probably didn't want to wake up next to me, but I didn't want you to be alone and scared when you woke up."

As she's trying to take this all in, she freaks out and tries to call Mel. She nearly falls on her face as she stumbles out of the bed. God, how much did he fucking give her? If I ever get my hands on him again— well, it just won't be pretty. He'll get a lot more than a knee to the sac.

"Shh. Don't freak out. It's okay. I texted her last night and let her know that you were here. Don't worry. It's all taken care of." I lean in close to her needing to touch her, to inhale her intoxicating smell. When the pad of my thumb traces over her face, across her lips, my groin twitches with the electricity that moves between us. In all of my experience, I have never gotten *this* excited from a simple touch. I'm lost in her beauty; she's mesmerizing and I'm completely disarmed by the charge between us.

"You were watching me?" Her question brings me out of my erotic musings about doing much more to her lips than just trace over them with my fingertip.

"Um…yeah. I guess you could say that. It's just …well…I didn't trust that guy. I'd never seen him there and he was staring at you like a wolf eyeing up a lamb while you were leaning over the pool table. I wanted to make sure that you were okay, that's all." Pulling my hand from her face, I readjust the sheets across my lap to hide my growing erection. I shouldn't be turned on as we sit here discussing her attempted attack, but I want her. Thinking about protecting her just makes me wish she was mine. That's what's turning me on. Her being mine and only mine.

When she thanks me for saving her, that desire grows even more. She might just be the sweetest girl

I've ever known. I only hear the tail end of what she's saying as I'm lost thinking about just how sweet—and hot, for that matter—she must taste. "…I know you don't really like me and all, so I just wanted to say thank you for helping me despite that."

Okay, wait a minute! Did I just hear her correctly? "That's what you think? You think I hate you?" I don't mean for my words to be harsh and biting, but they are. Here I am daydreaming about being with her and she thinks I hate her. Oh, she's got another thing coming to her.

"Well, I know I'm not your favorite person. That's for certain. I'd like to think you don't *hate* me, Reid, but I don't think you like me very much." I lean in as close as I can to her. I feel her breath on my lips and mine are no more than a millimeter from hers.

Cupping her cheek, and then grazing my knuckles across her soft skin, I say, "I definitely do not hate you." I can only hope and pray she hears the truth in my words.

"Then what is it Reid? What is going on here?" Cue the flailing hands again. "I'm exhausted from all of this. You antagonize me and all but treat me like shit, and then you run in like some kind of knight in shining armor to rescue me from some big bad wolf. I—I don't know what to do or how to feel. I can't keep running away from you. Avoiding you is draining me."

She's ranting and raving so quickly, that the deep breath she inhales, forces her chest out; I can't help but look down at her perfect tits.

"Since the moment I met you, I've wanted to be here in your arms, but you've done nothing but push me away. So tell me how I was supposed to think that you felt anything other than hatred for me." She finishes her little tirade and I quickly dart my eyes back to hers. There'd be no use in getting caught checking her out right now.

I need to change the mood here. We're good together when we're playful. It's easier to flirt than fight. "So you think I'm a knight in shining armor, huh?" I grin all goof-ball-like at her hoping that she'll slow down a bit and lighten up. When her hand falls playfully to my chest, the electricity returns. Her skin on mine is scorching hot. She looks down at her hand on my bare chest and her eyes widen with what I can only hope is desire.

We carry on the rest of the conversation basically laying out what an asshole I've been and how much I've hurt her. It's nothing I didn't already know, but I couldn't help it. I can't be the first guy on Earth who was ever afraid to admit his feelings to a girl before.

Yet, for the very first time in my life, I'm tired of it. I'm tired of keeping everyone away and I refuse to deny myself Maddy any longer. It's confession time.

"You've completely knocked me off my game. I've never met anyone like you and it scares the shit out of me. It's like you don't see me." She begins to say something and I softly press my fingers to her luscious lips to silence her. "You don't see me; you see straight through me. You see beyond the outside and it's like you see the me no one else sees. I saw it in your eyes that first night I met you and it knocked me on my ass. I was a goner, and since then, I guess I've just been trying to push you away."

She doesn't believe me. Why should she? I know I've been a shit, but I have to continue talking to try and convince her. I've never needed someone to believe me more than I need Maddy to believe me right now. "You're a smart-ass, and I love that you keep me on my toes. You are most definitely not like the other girls, and I love that, but it also scares me like nothing else. I haven't let anyone in for years and, well, with you, I feel like I want to give it a chance."

All I can do now is hope she'll accept my apology and give me a chance. I know it's the last thing I deserve, but maybe, by some act of God, I'll get an opportunity to redeem myself. I think I can be a good guy. I've never done it before, but for Maddy, I want to try.

BONUS SCENE #3

Alternate Point of View from Let Love Stay

When Reid meets Katie from Katie's POV

There he is. Yep, that's him. I'll never forget him. It's difficult to wipe away the memories of your very first crush, especially when pictures of him line your mantel.

Oh God! He's looking around the parking lot. Slouching down in the seat of my roommate's car, I pray to God that he doesn't see me. When he turns his back to the cars facing the coffee shop and struts through the door, my heart rate returns to normal.

Reid Connely. After countless attempts to get in touch with him, he's finally here. And now, suddenly, I have no clue what to say. I know what I have to tell him is going to turn his world upside down, but time isn't on my side. I have to tell him. He has to know.

Nervousness permeates every cell in my body as I reach for the handle. Fuck! I can't do this.

I need some moral support. Pulling my phone out of my pocket, I dial Megan, my roommate. Of course, because she's the best person ever, she picks up on the first ring.

"You can do this," she coaches from the other end before I can even get a word out.

Stammering nervously over my words, all I can come up with is, "But, what if—" before she cuts me off.

"There is no 'what if' here. You have to talk to him. He has to know. Put your big girl panties on and get your ass in there." I scan the interior of her Corolla, trying to find the hidden camera she must have. How the hell does she know I'm still in the car?

"How the hell—"

"Did I know you haven't even gotten out of the car yet? Because I've known you forever, that's how. And I've heard this story from every angle. You did the right thing by calling him, and now, he's finally doing the right thing by agreeing to meet you. Now, get your ass in there, talk to him and then call me as soon as you're done. Okay?"

"Okay. Okay. I can do this. Thanks for the pep talk. I'll call you in a bit," I sigh into the line, but don't hang up.

"And Katie…"

"Yeah, Meg."

"You're a good person for doing this and I love you. I'll talk to you soon." Her chipper voice makes me feel a little lighter, but I'm still nervous as hell to get this over with.

Hanging up with her, I feel a lump form in my throat and tears burn at my eyes. I hope to God she's right. I hope I'm doing the right thing. I hope in the end of this, that Reid doesn't hate me, and that I don't make an already shitty situation even shittier.

Stepping out into the parking lot, I pull my jacket around my chest. God, it is freaking cold out here. Yet, despite the chill in the air, I still find myself walking ever so slowly into the Starbucks where Reid is waiting for me.

When I finally get the courage to walk into the small campus café, my eyes land on Reid immediately. Standing in front of him, I swallow back my fear. Holding my hand out to him, I smile brightly and hope for the best.

"Hi. You must be Reid. I'm Katelyn Donovan," I say almost unevenly. When he stands, his frame towers over me and his chair screeches loudly on the floor. Intimidated, by his size and the noise, I shrink back from him a little, but keep my hand extended. Shaking his hand is awkward, but at least he didn't tell me to fuck off.

"Hi, Katelyn. It's…uh…it's good to meet you, I guess." His words come out sounding unnatural, uneasy, as if he's trying to conceal his true feelings. Okay, let's get on with this then.

I take my jacket off and drape it on the back of my chair and Reid takes his seat. The air is thick with awkward silence as we both avoid eye contact for as long as possible.

His deep and curt voice catches me off guard. "I'm going to grab another coffee. Can I get you anything?" he asks politely, even though I think polite is the last thing he wants to be.

All right, fine. Let's see how he reacts to this then. Looking over at the brightly colored chalkboard, I pretend as if I'm trying to make a huge decision about which caffeinated beverage I should have.

"Sure, I'll have a grande, soy vanilla latte, skinny with a shot of caramel syrup." Hmmm, take that. Maybe it'll help break some of this tension.

"Um, okay, but can you write that down," Reid snidely remarks after I tell him my order.

Oh, I can't help it; my eyes roll almost involuntarily. "I'm kidding. I'll have a regular coffee; milk and sugar is just fine." I really was just trying to lighten the mood a little. So much for that plan, I guess.

While he's over on the line getting our drinks, I get a text from Megan asking how things are going. I quickly type back a response that "things are going just swell. We're running away tonight and getting married."

Her reply, an eye-rolling smiley face, tells me my sarcastic response was successfully received.

When Reid slinks back into his chair and slides my drink in front of me, my nerves return. Still unable to come up with anything to say, I feel lame.

He says, "So."

And all I can come up with is a "so" in response.

Well, that went over like a lead balloon. Reid's features harden instantly and there's a palpable tension building in around us. Leaning menacingly close to me across the small table, he seethes, "I don't want to be rude, well actually, I do, but I won't. You're the one who's been calling me, who's got something to say to me, so if you don't start talking, then there's really no point in me being here."

I take a small sip of my coffee in the hopes it will strengthen my resolve. It doesn't, but he's right. I'm the one who wanted this. I need to say something.

"You're right. I'm sorry. I am the one who wanted to talk and here I am all clammed up. I actually sat in the parking lot for about fifteen minutes before I came in. I just don't know where to start." Rubbing my hands over my legs in the hopes of warming them up is futile. My heart is racing, but the blood refuses to warm my extremities. Perhaps it has something to do with the icy atmosphere of this conversation.

One more sip and here we go. "Can I ask you something first?" I can see a whole swirl of anger move across his face at my question.

I reach to my side and tug my jacket across my lap. Twisting the string of my hoodie around my fingers, I say, "It'll help me figure out where to start." He doesn't answer my question; he just shoots me a look that I think means I should continue.

The point of the last few weeks, of all of those phone calls was to arrive at this one question. Thinking back over everything that has led me to this exact moment is so overwhelming—so much so, that I can't even spit out anything intelligible at first.

When I let my emotions settle, I finally ask, "When is the last time you spoke with your mom?"

My emotions might have just been checked, but Reid's, well to say he's angry is a huge understatement. I guess I should have expected that. You can't go digging into someone's past, especially a past as dark as his, and not expect anger in return.

BONUS SCENE #4

Alternate Point of View from Let Love Stay

The reunion scene from Maddy's POV

Thank God, this day is over. I thought office work would be somewhat easy, but my feet are killing me and my hands are all chapped and cut up from touching the files all day. Kathy calls out from the front office, "Come on girls! Let's get a move on. It's closing time."

Nikki comes up behind me as I'm gathering my stuff out of my small locker in the break room. We've hit it off really well this week and I'm really glad to have such nice co-workers. It makes the day move a lot quicker.

"So what are your plans tonight, Maddy? A few of the girls and I are heading to the club. Wanna come with us?" I so want to say yes, I really do. Getting all dolled up and dancing the night away with the girls, sounds like the perfect way to let go of some of this tension.

"Nikki, I wish I could, but I already have plans." I refuse to call it a date. It is *not* a date. Well, it might be if you ask Jay, but in my mind, it is most certainly not a date.

She's peering out the window as she says, rather cheerfully, "Oh yeah? Do your *plans* have anything to do with Mr. Hunkity Hunk in the parking lot." I have to laugh. She has this weird creative thing where she makes every hot guy's name into some cute Mr. Something-Or-Other. Just the other day she called the Fed-Ex guy Mr. Schmexy McSexy. Okay, that one wasn't all that creative, but I think she was a little flustered.

Walking over to the window, I glance at the freshly dubbed Mr. Hunkity Hunk and my stomach drops.

It's Jay.

Just when I think I can walk away unscathed, without having to explain anything to Nikki, Jay sees me in the window and waves up at us. Yeah, so much for that.

Nikki drapes her arms over my shoulders and waves back at him. "So who is he?" she asks, her voice all proud that she's just discovered something about my plans.

Huffing at her, I try to defend myself. "It's not a date. He's my ex. We're just getting dinner."

Tapping her finger to her bottom lip, she looks up to the ceiling pretending she's lost in deep thought. When her eyes return to me, they're alight with playfulness. "So let me get this straight. You used to date Hunkity Hunk down there who," she peers out the window, "is still smiling and waving up here like a fool in love. You're going out to dinner with said Hunkity Hunk, but it's not a date."

"No, it is most definitely not a date!" My attempts at self-defense are just making me look guiltier. I huff again and try to walk away.

"Okay. Okay. But Maddy, promise me one thing," she asks, serious all of a sudden.

I stand and wait impatiently for what I just know will be a pointless question.

"Promise you'll call me the instant you get home from your non-date to let me know how it went."

We both share a laugh at her ridiculousness as we make our way to the front where everyone else is waiting to leave for the day.

Walking out into the frigid winter air, I pull my jacket around me. Jay catches sight of me right away and walks over to me.

Pulling me into hug, he says, "I'm so glad you agreed to come out with me. You look beautiful, Maddy."

I can't help but roll my eyes at his compliments. I look anything but good and that was the point. My hair is in a sloppy ponytail and my make-up hasn't been touched since early this morning. A disheveled, hot mess is probably more along the lines of what I look like.

Suddenly, Jay's eyes widen a bit more and he seems to be staring off in the distance behind me.

Curious to see whatever has caught his attention, I turn around and my stomach drops again.

It's Reid.

My pulse skyrockets. My heart careens into my ribcage. My palms get sweaty. My desire surges.

Before I can say or do anything, Jay pushes me behind him and eyes Reid up and down. I want to warn him, tell him to just leave Reid alone, but my brain and my mouth will not function.

Stepping into Reid's face, Jay says, "Who the fuck are you? What do you want?" Oh God. Reid is going to punch him. I know it. I can see vivid images of Reid laying Logan flat on his ass and I want to step in the middle of them, to protect Jay and embrace Reid, but my goddamn feet are stuck to the floor.

I can't believe he's here.

Locking my eyes with his magnetic blue depths, I try to convey my love for him, my apologies for this scene that I can only imagine he's misreading.

"Me? I'm the boyfriend, asshole." Reid bites out a few choice words to Jay, but his eyes are glued to mine.

His voice soothes my tattered soul. It makes my insides clench and my heart soar. He's really here.

Jay's voice breaks through to my distracted state. "I'm Maddy's date for tonight. You know? She never mentioned a boyfriend when I asked her out. Must not be much of a boyfriend if she doesn't even mention you." Oh God, no he didn't! Just as I'm about to speak up and stop the inevitable onslaught I know he will bring, I watch Reid effortlessly drop Jay to his ass.

Standing over him and holding him up by his collar, Reid barks into Jay's face, "Whether she mentioned me or not, she's mine, so lay the fuck off. Got it?"

I'm his? Does that mean that he's mine?

Reid reaches out his hand to mine and my mind is swirling with so much confusion that my brain isn't firing correctly. When I finally put two-and-two together and reach out for him, I see him visibly relax. Fire and electricity travel from his hand straight to my heart and I feel like I'm home again.

In a freezing cold dentist's office parking lot, I finally feel like I'm home again.

BONUS SCENE #5

Deleted Scene from Let Love Stay

Christmas shopping - Maddy's POV

I hate Christmas shopping. I was never a fan of giving or receiving gifts. Aunt Maggie never gave me more than knitting needles and yarn. All she ever got in return was a gift card to the local craft store. She was happy and I was miserable, but hell, that was just how life was.

Holding some lame-ass pair of flannel pajama pants up in front me, I smile all too happily at the thought of these hanging low on Reid's hips. Yes, these will do just fine.

Mel chimes in from across the rack at Macy's. "What's the goofy grin for?"

"Huh? Oh me? Nothing?"

"Don't 'Oh nothing' me, Missy! You were so just mentally drooling all over your boyfriend, weren't you?"

Guiltily, I place the pants back on the rack and laugh at her. "Okay, fine I was…daydreaming. But can you blame me?"

"Eww, no. I am so not weighing in on how hot Reid is! He's like a brother. Eww. No. Gross." Melanie is flailing her arms all over the place and holding her nose in a mock protest of how stinky she thinks this conversation is.

Walking up next to her and wrapping my arm around her shoulder, I hug her tightly. "Methinks the lady doth protest too much," I quote and she just smacks my arm playfully.

"Okay, fine. He's hot, but marginally so." Melanie arches her eyebrow at me and I know I've won.

We walk out of Macy's, no purchases in hand and I'm really struggling with what to get him. As we're walking down the overly crammed walkway of the mall, I'm instantly drawn to the pretzel stand at the side. Buttery, doughy goodness? Yes, please!

After handing the cashier my money, I lean back on the counter and wait for my drink and pretzel nuggets. I catch Melanie staring across the way, and following her persistent gaze, my stomach drops when I see Reid in the jewelry store.

Grabbing onto her, I nearly rip Melanie's arm out of the socket. "Is that…is he…he's not buying…" I can't even get a full sentence out.

Melanie's face is laced with surprise as she turns to face me. "I don't know, Maddy. Do you want me to go talk to him?"

"I don't know! What are you going to say? Don't tell him I'm here! Oh God!" Melanie laughs at my overly dramatic reaction.

"Oh, just calm down, would you! I'll just say I saw him and thought maybe he could use some help. Okay?" She runs her hands down my arms to try and calm me down. It doesn't work.

Slinking down into one of the chairs the pretzel booth has set up, I prop my bag up in front of me to try and disguise myself. All I really manage to do is feel like an idiot. I'm sure I look like an idiot too.

Watching from behind my stupid bag like a moron, I watch Melanie and Reid chatting animatedly. She points at something and Reid points at another.

When Reid turns away to pay the clerk, Melanie looks over to me and stifles a laugh. She holds her hands out in front of her and mouths the words "it's huge."

My heart plummets. She didn't let him buy what I think he just bought, did she?

Now, I sound like a fool even in my own head.

As Melanie walks back over to me, I see Reid walk the other way. Standing up from behind my post, I nearly yell at her as she approaches. "What the hell, Melanie? What did you just do? Please tell me you didn't—" She cuts me off before I can continue my frenzy.

"Oh, just shut up." She quips as she grabs her bag and mine from the table. Saying nothing else, she just walks away from me.

Chasing after her like the fool that I am, I call out, "What did he buy me? Where are you going? Melanie!" The last shrill outcry forces her to turn around. It also garners a few awkward stares from some shoppers.

"Oh.My.God. I am not telling you what he bought you." She crosses her arms over her chest and snickers at me. "But, believe me, you'll love it." When her lips curl up into the goofiest grin, I want to slap it off her face.

Pulling me to her side, she smiles, "I think we're going to have to do better than flannel PJs though."

That thought makes my stomach drop yet again.

BONUS SCENE #6

Deleted Scene from Let Love Stay

Ice Cream - Reid's POV

"What about this one?" I hold a random carton of ice cream in front of me. Picking out an ice cream flavor should not be *this* difficult.

Leave it to Maddy though.

Holding the pint of Ben and Jerry's, she's actually reading the label. "Maddy! Does it really matter? It's chocolate. It's peanut butter. What else could you want? Let's just get this one." I wrap my arms around her waist and nuzzle into her neck. I know what'll get her ass in gear. "The sooner we get home," I lick her neck to emphasize my point, "the sooner we can start the movie. And the sooner we start the movie, well, then," one more lick just to bring the point home, "the sooner we can get distracted by other things." I shove certain "other things" into her fine, tight ass just to continue emphasizing my point.

Damn! Now I want to get out of here for entirely different reasons.

I feel her melt against me and I know I've won.

"Hmmm," is the only response of which she's capable.

The superhero fanatic in me fist pumps in the air. I have been dying to see the new Batman movie since it came out on DVD, but well, even when you put Batman up against hot sex with your girl, well, sex always wins.

Walking hand in hand to the cashier, Maddy stares up at me dreamily. "I know what we could do instead of watching one of your silly 'boy movies'." She arches an eyebrow at me and I know exactly what she means. She's not getting off that easily. Well, I mean she will, eventually. But, dammit, I'm watching my movie first.

I pull her to my side as we walk away from the cashier. "Oh, no you don't! The last time we rented this DVD, you won."

She huffs a sigh at me. "What the heck is that supposed to mean, 'I won?'" Her words are shocked, but playfully so. She knows exactly what I mean.

As we walk up to the car, I open the door for her and lean into her neck once again. "You know exactly what I mean. Now, if you let me watch my movie *first*," I lick a seductive path from her neck up to her jawline and hover above her lips. When I've rendered her speechless, I move my lips to speak at they flutter on top of her. "Well, if you let me watch this first, then you'll win over and over and over again."

Her responding groan is all I need to hear to know I've won. Boy movie night it is. Not to be overshadowed by "the hottest sex of your life" sex night either.

※※*

In true Maddy fashion, she passed out on my lap less than thirty minutes into the movie. That works out perfectly for me actually. I got to watch the movie, and now, I get to carry a drowsy Maddy up to her room and, well, you know.

She barely stirs as I move to pick her up, but by the time I'm halfway up the stairs, she finally wakes up.

"Did I miss the movie?" she asks sleepily while pressing her lips against my neck.

"You sure did, sweetheart. But don't worry, we can watch it again tomorrow night." My response is met with a playful swat to the ass.

I didn't even realize her hand was back there!

As I drop her onto the bed, she looks up at me lustfully. Oh, hell! Two can play at that game. I feign a yawn and plop down next to her. "I'm beat, Maddy. Let's go to sleep." Trying my best to hide my smile, I turn on my side and curl away from her.

I can hear her harrumph and fidget on the bed. Before I can say or do anything, she's pinching me on the side, tickling the shit out of me. Oh it's on now!

With lightning quick reflexes, I turn over to her and wrap my legs around hers, essentially pinning her in place. "So that's how you want to play it, huh?" I pull her arms above her head and encircle both of her tiny wrists in one of my hands.

Her eyes dilate and I can see how hard she has to work to swallow past her desire. Just when I have her where I want her, I reach for her breast with my other hand.

Hovering above her supple flesh, I wink at her and then change tactics quickly. Pinching and tickling at her sides and underarms has her squirming beneath me in seconds.

"Reid…stop…please… that tickles…" Her words trail off into a fit of hysterical laughter.

When she's out of breath, I press my lips softly to hers and stare into her deep green eyes. "Love you, babe."

"I love you, too, Reid. Now, can we finally go to sleep?" She arches her hips up into mine on the word "sleep" and I know "sleep" is the last thing either one of us have planned.

BONUS SCENE #7

Character interview with Maddy and Reid

This character interview was done for the Let Love Stay Blog tour with Lisa Jones at True Story Book Blog.

I'm very excited to get to meet Reid and Maddy from Let Love In/Let Love Stay. I heart them big time—they're like a life size Barbie and Ken doll. I arrive at the local coffee shop where we decided to meet, and walk in to find them already seated at a small bistro table near the back. Perfect, nice and quiet so I can pick their brains without being disturbed.

They rise to greet me shaking my hand. They're both so warm and friendly and couldn't look any happier. Gives me butterflies! They're soooo cute!

Lisa: "Well, I know you both are very busy, so if you don't mind, I guess we'll jump right in."

Reid: "Sounds good to us."

Maddy looks over to me smiling and nodding in agreement.

Lisa: "So, Reid, what do you think Shane would think about Maddy?"

Reid looks over and smiles warmly at Maddy.

Reid: "He'd love her. Hell, he'd have a partner in crime with her."

Maddy grabs his hand and lovingly squeezes. Awww… I give them both a warm smile.

Lisa: "Personally, I thought your old car was pretty sweet. Do you miss your mustang?"

Reid: "Hell, yeah, that car was awesome. Had lots of good memories in that car."

His voice is positively cocky. Maddy gives him a sideways glance and he quickly straightens in his chair.

Reid: "Um, what I meant to say is no. No, I don't miss that car one bit."

Nice recovery, Reid.

Lisa: "How is work going? Everything you thought it would be?"

Reid's face splits into a mega-watt, panty-dropping smile.

Reid: "It's freaking great. I've actually been meeting with this one kid lately and he reminds me so much of Shane it's scary. I met him at a presentation we did at a local high school, and he's been coming to The Bridge for a few weeks now. I really hope to help him out. Oh, and working with Dylan every day is great too. It's like I got back a piece of my family when he came back."

I think the biggest reason why that smile is panty dropping is because it's genuine. You can hear the joy in his voice.

Lisa: "Biggest regret?"

As Reid rubs his hands nervously over his thighs, his eyes search the ceiling for an answer.

Reid: "My mom. I just wish I had more time with her."

Maddy reaches over and places her hand over his chest, where his tattoo is inked. Looking down at Maddy's hand, Reid instinctively reaches his up to encompass hers. It's very touching...makes my little heart squeeze.

Lisa: "All right Miss. Madeleine, it's your turn!"

She gives me a big smile.

Maddy: "I'm ready."

Lisa: "What do you think your parents would think about Reid?"

Maddy: "I think my dad would have hated him at first!"

Reid swats her on the arm jokingly.

Reid: "Hey! I'm not that bad, am I?"

Maddy: "No, silly! I just mean that when we first met, you were pretty much every father's worst nightmare. Now, well, now you're a dream come true."

She speaks the truth!

Lisa: "Can you imagine your life without Momma and Mel?"

Maddy: "Not one bit. I don't know what ever made me think they weren't my family. Momma stops over a few times a week to visit Braden. She loves that little boy like he's her own. She makes me miss my mom just a little bit less."

Aww…

Lisa: "Do you still have plans to go back to college?"

Maddy: "Absolutely. I signed up for night classes as soon as I moved back home. It was a difficult decision to leave Mel and the girls back at Ithaca, but things have a funny way of working out."

Lisa: "Good for you! What's your biggest regret?"

Maddy: "Pushing Reid away in the hospital."

Reid drapes his arm around Maddy's shoulder and kisses the top of her head. Placing her hand on his knee, she squeezes gently and continues.

Maddy: "I should know better than anyone that people react to things in their own way. It wasn't fair, but at the time it was a defense mechanism, I guess. But it brought him closure with his mom and we made it work in the end, so I guess I can't regret it too much."

Lisa: "As long as it worked out, that's what matters. All right, now it's time for both of you at the same time – what are your favorite five things about the other – physical and non-physical"
;-)

Maddy: "Hmmm, non-physical, let's see: he's smart and caring. He cooks, because Lord knows I can't. He's an amazing dad and he makes me laugh. Physical, ehhh, I guess he's okay."

They both laugh but then Maddy flushes and her cheeks turn pink. She's so cute.

Maddy: "I'll keep it PG-13 and say – his hands, his lips, his arms, his eyes and his tattoos."

Lisa: "Hmm…good answers!"

Reid's eyes rake over Maddy's body from head to toe.

Reid: "Yeah, there's only one thing I can come up with physically."

A shocked look flits across Maddy's face as she hits him on the chest.

Maddy: "Only one?"

Reid: "Yep, just one. EVERYTHING!"

He has a huge shit-eating grin as he kisses the tip of her nose and she smiles brightly back at him.

Reid: "And non-physical, yeah, I'm going to say EVERYTHING again."

Maddy: "See, I told you he was smart!"

I didn't think it was possible for Maddy to smile any bigger than she already was.

Lisa: "What's your biggest pet peeve?"

Maddy: "When other girls hit on him. I mean, I'm right there, with his kid no less. I mean come on!"

Reid tries to stifle his laughter, but when a chuckle slips out, Maddy crosses her arms across her chest.

Reid: "Sorry about that, babe. I can't help it if they all want me."

Maddy shrugs her shoulders, and allows Reid to pull her into his side in an embrace.

Maddy: "Whatever. I get to bring you home at night. They can look all they want."

Tapping his finger to his bottom lip, Reid looks like he's thinking carefully about his response.

Reid: "I would have to say my biggest pet peeve is blind hatred. It brings me back to all of the things that Shane and Dylan, and too many other people have gone through. There's no reason to hate someone over who they love."

Lisa: "Very insightful, Reid. I have to agree with Maddy; you are pretty smart. You've had an 'unconventional' relationship from the start. Was there an 'ah-ha' moment when you 'knew' that this was the only person for you or was it gradual?"

They both look at each other and answer at the same time.

Maddy: "Gradual."

Reid: "Instantly."

Maddy gapes over at him with a "you have got to be kidding me" face.

Maddy: "Seriously? You were all douche-tastic in the beginning!"

Reid's face sobers a bit and he sits up straighter in his seat.

Reid: "Yeah, I'm not proud of that. But it was because I knew right away you were different. I'm not too macho to say it scared me and I acted like an ass."

Lisa: "Well, at least you can admit that now. And speaking of admitting–re-do time! The night at the hospital, what would each of you have done differently?"

Reid: "I never would have walked out."

Maddy: "I never would have pushed him away."

Lisa: "Alright, I've been too serious–kinky question time! :-P Have you had more fun with using the belt from Maddy's robe?" *Lol*

I can't help but giggle as I watch Maddy slink down into her chair and her face turn red. Reid sits up proudly and his lips curl into a sexy, lopsided grin. No one says anything.

Lisa: "Alright…maybe too kinky! We'll move on! Where do you see yourselves in the next five years?"

Reid: "I'd like to finally buy that house I promised her. She deserves a white picket fence and all that stuff."

Reid's chest puffs with pride as he smiles at Maddy and she beams back at him. Gah…they're just so stinkin' cute.

Maddy: "I'm perfect where we are, but I'd like to be done with school. Maybe another kid."

Reid smiles and pulls her close.

Lisa: "Okay, time for some word association. Give me the first thing that comes to mind. Family?"

Maddy and Reid answer at the same time: "Braden"

Aww…it's cute and dorky and sweet and they turn to each other and share a small kiss.

Lisa: "Shane?"

Reid almost subconsciously rubs the scar on his chin.

Reid: "Pain."

Maddy: "Dylan."

Lisa: "Trust?"

Reid: "Maddy."

Maddy: "Melanie."

Looking at Reid, I say,

Lisa: "Maddy?"

Reid: "Perfect."

I grin and nod, and turn to Maddy,

Lisa: "Reid?"

Maddy: "Happily ever after."

I think I might get a toothache from all the cuteness and sweetness – but I still love it.

Lisa: "Love?"

Reid: "Her."

Maddy: "Possible."

Lisa: "Very good answers! Ya'll are surprising me a little bit. Now for some rapid fire questions. It's really easy, either/or, just pick one…fast or slow?"

Maddy: "Slow.

Reid: "Slow…THEN fast."

Kinky…I like it! ;-)

Lisa: "Books or movies?"

Maddy: "My Kindle"

Smart Girl!

Reid: "Not chick flicks."

Such a boy!

Lisa: "Muscle cars or jeeps?"

Maddy: "Jeep"

Reid: "Jeep. You'd be surprised how much room is in the back when you fold the seat down!"

Kinky again! Love it! :-D   Maddy blushes and gives him a love tap. He kisses the top of her head as she buries her face in his shirt. She's so cute when she is embarrassed.

Lisa: "Chocolate or vanilla?"

Maddy: "Chocolate"

Reid: "Vanilla."

He winks and adds,

Reid: "As long as I get to keep the robe belt."

I think the reddish-hue on Maddy's cheeks might be permanent!

Lisa: "Hot or cold?"

Together: "HOT!"

We all share a laugh at their enthusiastic, in-unison response.

Lisa: "Go out or stay in?"

Reid: "Stay in. I love coming home to my family at the end of the day."

Awwww…

Maddy: "And we love when you come home. I say 'in' too."

Bigger Awwwww!

Lisa: "Hard or soft?"

Maddy: "Both. As long as it's with him, I'll take it every way I can."

Reid: "What she said!"

*Yup, it has been confirmed. I love them to bits and pieces. We stay and chat for a while. I try and get the scoop from Maddy about Mel, but she is sadly tight lipped. Going to make me wait. *sigh* Of course, Reid is enjoying telling me loads of stories about Braden—such a proud daddy…so freakin' cute and makes him that much more drool-worthy. I don't even realize how long we've been talking until I glance at my phone and realize we've been there for over two hours just chatting. I give them both hugs and we say our goodbyes and I watch them walk off hand-in-hand.*